WHAT PEOPLE

TO THE DEVIL'S TUNE

This thought-provoking story had us hooked from the first page, and is something that will resonate with you long after the last page. An inspiring tale about one woman's strength, courage and empowering journey to self-love, it's a touching story with a very powerful message – we couldn't put it down!
Soul&Spirit Magazine

With endearing characters, based on real people who have told their personal stories to Jo, this novel will appeal to anyone who enjoys a heart warming read about personal growth through adversity. Drawing from her own skills as an experienced healer and teacher, Jo lovingly and carefully brings serious, hard hitting issues into the story, teaming them with real life solutions, which makes it a moving, helpful and empowering read. Some books leave you hanging; *To The Devil's Tune* leaves you with hope.
Chrissie Astell, best selling author, teacher & facilitator

A mixture of trepidation and excitement welled over me as Jo's manuscript *To The Devil's Tune* landed on my doorstep. Just like temptation itself; what on Earth was I going to find inside these pages? What I found was well, yes, addictive, truly addictive, and a journey through Hell, in the most enjoyable way! The name Lucifer means light bringer, and Jo brings the light here, a self help book, but written in the style of Mills and Boon… Truly addictive – and enlightening.
Tiffany Crosara, award winning author & TV psychic

For a début novel, this is, in my opinion, an outstanding piece of work. I know how difficult it can be to keep motivated, to find the drive to continue and I applaud the work Jo has put into this book.

Knowing Jo, her background and her ethos on life, I can see her personality shining through this book. She has handled each page with care and consideration, ensuring that you want to continue reading "just another page".

I wish Jo every success with this book and I encourage her, from the bottom of my heart, to write more. She has a voice, she has passion and it would be a crime for her not to continue with a whole series.

Lynn Nicholson, editor of *The International Lifestyle Magazine*

To the Devil's Tune

To the Devil's Tune

Jo Barnard

Winchester, UK
Washington, USA

First published by Roundfire Books, 2014
Roundfire Books is an imprint of John Hunt Publishing Ltd., Laurel House, Station Approach,
Alresford, Hants, SO24 9JH, UK
office1@jhpbooks.net
www.johnhuntpublishing.com
www.roundfire-books.com

For distributor details and how to order please visit the 'Ordering' section on our website.

Text copyright: Jo Barnard 2013

ISBN: 978 1 78279 629 9

A CIP catalogue record for this book is available from the British Library.

Design: Stuart Davies

Printed in the USA by Edwards Brothers Malloy

We operate a distinctive and ethical publishing philosophy in all
areas of our business, from our global network of authors to
production and worldwide distribution.

For Olive, in loving memory xxx

Acknowledgements

Thank you to the two friends who were kind and brave enough to bare their souls in order that I share their true stories with you.

Thanks also to my loving family who supported me in my 'NaNoWriMo' challenge to write this, my debut novel, in the space of one month.

Chapter One

I couldn't bear the feeling of helplessness any longer. Something had to give. It felt like my head and chest had merged to form one giant pressure cooker, and I needed to release some steam. There was only one thing that could help me to escape this torture, and that meant allowing all this pain inside of me to come out.

As the familiar panic began to rise, I reached for my tweezers and began to pick away at the fresh scab on my ankle. As I used more and more pressure, and watched the blood rise to the surface and trickle down my foot, my heartache slowly began to subside. I felt alive, and totally in the moment.

The loud ring of my mobile startled me. Heart racing, I looked at the clock. It was just before eight. I reached for my phone, wondering who'd be calling me at this time in the morning; deeply wishing it was him. But glancing at the flashing screen, I could see it was Saffie. Without hesitation, I answered.

"Morning, Jude!" Her voice sounded panicky.

"Hey, Saff. Everything ok? You sound harassed."

"Having one of those mornings, honey! Sol's running a fever and I really need to stay home with him today. I can't drag him in to the shop all shivery. You wouldn't be a complete sweetheart and open up for me would you? Of course, I'll pay you the extra."

What could I say? Aside from the fact I could really use the money right now, Saffie was an absolute angel to work for, and the fact that someone needed me somehow lifted my spirits and brought me back round.

"I'll be there in half an hour. Give Sol a big kiss from me. Tell him that 'Auntie Judith' sends him healing hugs and magical well-wishes."

I wasn't really his auntie, and rarely did I admit to people that my real name was Judith, but I'd come to know Saffie so well, that I was comfortable to mock myself in front of her. She was the gentlest, most genuine person I knew. But how unfair that her parents had given her an exotic and beautiful name like Safiyah, meaning 'purity', whereas mine had settled on Judith! I remember romantically looking up the meaning of my name when I was eleven, only to find:

Judith – A biblical name, meaning 'Jewness'.

Having never been one for religion, rules or rigid structure of any kind, I quickly decided that from then on, I'd introduce myself simply as 'Jude', meaning 'praise'. Sweeter and more enchanting for this here creative spirit, I thought.

"'Auntie Judith', you're a complete darling!" Saffie said, relieved, a smile in her voice. "I'll call you later."

I cleaned up my bloody wound, disguising it ashamedly beneath a pair of thick black tights. Fortunately, the colder months allowed me to cover up without too much cause for suspicion.

Hurting myself wasn't something I was proud of, but it seemed like the lesser of two evils when things got bad. At the time it felt so satisfying; a way of venting my frustration. And right now, it was much easier to deal with external wounds than internal ones. That's the problem when you feel alone.

I'd come to the conclusion that men just couldn't be with me for long. Even though I really loved them, sure enough, they'd find a way to leave me. Maybe it was something I said or did without even realising. I wished I could figure it out, but I couldn't. All I really understood was how alone I felt.

I brushed my long hair and plaited it to the side. I loved trying out new boho styles; pretty braids here and there, but right now, I needed something quick as I had to get out of the door sharpish. I liquid-lined my lashes, cherry-glossed my lips, and put on a short, sequinned, Indian-style dress which looked quite cute over my thick tights. No one would ever notice the fresh wound that was throbbing away painfully beneath.

It didn't take much to make my tiny flat look untidy. I hadn't lived there long; only a few months. But I'd made it my own, surrounding myself with all the things I loved; artwork (most of which was mine), silk throws, wall hangings, wooden carvings, and the large collection of crystals I'd accumulated over the past few years. These items of beauty, teamed with the heady smell of incense, brought some comfort to my awful situation.

I liked to keep it nice; a tranquil sanctuary to retreat to, but with no time to spare today, I closed the door behind me, leaving the mess for later. At least the painful images of Matt weren't so intense now.

* * *

We'd first met in a bar when I was twenty-six, and as soon as I saw him I knew he was the type of guy that my dreams were made of. His eyes were mesmerising; like pools of crystal blue.

I was out with the girls that night, and was just returning from the ladies' to buy a round of drinks at the bar when our eyes connected. It's hard to explain, but at that moment, something ignited within me – like I'd suddenly woken up to a new life on a whole different level. Thinking back, our entire meeting was dreamlike.

The attraction was definitely mutual, and we spent the rest of the evening chatting away at complete ease and gazing intently into one another's eyes, much to the dismay of my girlfriends. When last orders were called, I felt sick to the stomach at the thought of never seeing this man again, and so with a great confidence that I had never felt before, I invited him back to my place for a coffee.

Sweeping my hair gently behind my ear, he leant towards me

and whispered, "Well...if you're sure...then I'd really love that." The warmth of his breath on my neck, together with the firm intent of his words, filled me with a powerful excitement that rocked every part of me. As my front door closed behind us, our foreheads connected. And in this literal meeting of minds, it was clear that we both ached for the same thing.

With no need for words, he pulled my body close to his. An incredible rush of heady excitement surged through me. His large hands encased my tiny waist, encircling my core, leaving no room for manoeuvre (although, quite frankly, I couldn't think of anywhere I'd rather be). After an intense gaze, his lips met mine, tenderly at first, stopping between each gentle kiss, allowing us time to steady ourselves before what we both knew was to come. As we tasted each other, he began to press closer, gently teasing me with his hardness, his intense expression holding me completely and keeping this powerful connection strong.

I remembered the cloudy, heady feeling; almost heavenly; how it seemed as though the two of us had melted, merged and morphed into one bright light. I'd never wanted anyone as much as I wanted this man right now, and I felt so alive.

Unable to contain ourselves for a second longer, we undressed each other, almost in a panic; desperate for our entire bodies to meet skin to skin before it was too late. And when his hard masculinity met my warm femininity, he fitted me like a glove, and it didn't take long before we reached, and revelled in, a heady state of euphoria, savouring every moment, and moaning with pleasure for some time after.

From that moment on, I knew I wouldn't be satisfied until I knew everything there was to know about this man. Absolutely everything.

* * *

I tried to smile at the customer as I gift-wrapped her hand-carved wooden elephant. My ankle was throbbing; pulsating with pain beneath my tights. I'd struggled to bear any weight on it all day. Still, only an hour to go before I finished, and I knew there was a quaint little tea shop only a few doors down that I could sit in for a while. I'd take some painkillers and let them work their magic before walking home again.

Although working in a gift shop wasn't exactly rocket science, I enjoyed the loving vibe of the place, and being surrounded by such objects of beauty was always a joy. Not only did it just about pay the bills, I felt comfortable and safe working there, and that suited me down to the ground. And at least one day a week, Saffie would take the day off, leaving me in charge to manage the shop, paying me extra which I was always grateful for. Today was one of those days, albeit unexpected, but I needed every penny. The perks were good too; free incense and candles whenever we took a new delivery, which helped keep my flat cosy, and hugs on demand. Saffie was warm and generous like that.

With not a customer in sight, I flicked through a TV guide that had been left on the side. A cosy night in with some good telly was just about all I could manage tonight. I noticed that the movie *Annie* was on at seven. I so loved the uplifting spirit of that film. If an orphan child could make the best of life, then maybe I could too. But it all seemed so impossible.

Humming the 'Tomorrow' song, I dusted the shelves and cashed up, taking my wage from the till, and locking the shop carefully behind me before heading off to take the weight off my feet. I ordered a large frothy latte and took a seat on a small table in the back corner of the tea shop. No one would notice me there, and I'd be left alone to drink my coffee in peace, and think back.

What was it with me and men, I wondered? Was it something I said or did that pushed them away? Or was I living under some sort of unavoidable karmic past-life curse perhaps? All I knew was that I just wanted to be loved and cherished, and to love and cherish in return. But where were Matt and Dad in my hour of need; those two men that I had loved and adored so much?

"Large latte?" asked the waitress, placing my coffee down in front of me. No doubt she had a gorgeous man in tow; one who loved her completely and was there for the keeps, I imagined.

"Oh, yes, thanks," I replied quietly, leaning forward to help, trying not to bend my ankle in the process. I immersed my lips in the warm froth, wrapping both hands around the large cup, and imagining how it would feel to live a normal, happy life, whatever that was.

From the corner of my eye, I saw a tall woman approach my little table. So much for not wanting to be disturbed, I thought. The vision of her advance brought me fully back into the here and now, snapping me out of my woeful muse. "Do you mind if I borrow the sugar pot please, darling?" she asked. "I've never been sweet enough you see! I'll bring it straight back."

"Oh, of course, go ahead," I replied, trying to muster a smile. I suddenly realised how good this coffee tasted, its sweetness and warmth bringing momentary comfort to my solitary darkness. Had I been able to afford another, I would've gulped it down, but I couldn't, so I sipped it slowly and returned to my reflections.

Sure enough, the woman returned. Her clothes were bright, as was her lipstick and rouge, and teamed with her tall stature, forthright walk, and steely grey hair, you couldn't miss her even if you wanted to. As she placed the sugar pot back down on the table, she leant towards me and said in a low but friendly voice, "Someone looks like they don't like themselves very much today." Her sense of perception took me by surprise. I became acutely aware of my face beginning to redden.

As she loomed above me, I knew she had more to say. It was crystal clear that my lack of response was not going to stop her from continuing, so I looked up at her, our eyes making contact. I can't explain, but I felt strangely drawn to this woman.

"I know it's none of my business, but believe me, darling, life is too short to carry burdens around with you; it really is. Anyway, I hope I haven't offended you. I'll leave you alone now, but if you ever want to share it…"

With that, she placed a slip of paper down next to my hand and returned to her friends. I glanced down. Written elaborately in blue fountain ink, reminding me of my grandmother's handwriting, was the name 'Annie', together with a local phone number. How bizarre, I thought, that this lady could so clearly sense my sadness; even though I thought I disguised it pretty well. And odder still, that she was prepared to listen to the problems of a complete stranger. What was all that about?

Feeling slightly embarrassed and somewhat exposed, I hurriedly paid for my latte, slipping the paper into my jacket pocket. The woman and I made no eye contact, but I was somehow struck by how wonderfully happy she was. And also that she already had a sugar pot on her table.

As I limped home, my ankle feeling swollen and bruised, I realised that, for the first time in ages, I didn't feel quite so alone.

Chapter Two

I guess it all began when I was nine. The pain, that is. Looking back after all these years, I still remember it as clear as anything.

It was a warm, sticky day at the end of June, and the sound of the school bell, ringing home time, was music to my ears. I was looking forward to telling Dad about the wildlife project we'd just started. Dad loved talking about nature, and I knew he'd be able to offer some useful information that I could impress the class with tomorrow.

He was never much help with maths or literacy, but when it came to nature, my dad was the man. Plants, flowers, animals; anything to do with the earth really, was what he took pleasure from. His other passion was talking about his Scottish heritage; something he was extremely proud of, and which made him feel connected to his homeland. He was a gentle soul, my dad; very sweet, with a real innocence about him. Quite childlike I guess, in many ways.

Mum came to collect us from school as usual; *us* meaning me and my big sister, Deborah. Deb was only a year older than me, but she was my big sister nonetheless. This was her final year at our primary school. Before long, I'd have to stand on my own two feet, without the love of my big sister to watch out for me. Not that I needed it of course, but it always felt good just knowing she was there.

Deb met me at my classroom door, and as usual, we held hands as we ran to the school gates, where Mum would be waiting for us. And there she was. Just like any other day. Or so we thought...

"Hi, girls!" she said. "Here, let me carry your bags for you. I thought we could walk home via the shop today, get you an ice cream or something. Special treat."

What had we done to deserve this, we wondered. And it

wasn't even the weekend! Nonetheless, we nodded enthusiastically at her suggestion.

All in all, Mum was a kind woman. She didn't have too many friends, but that was through choice really. Mum kept herself to herself. Nevertheless, she was polite and neighbourly, and would gladly help anyone in need. As well as having a couple of cleaning jobs, she helped out in the local charity shop once a week, sifting through people's donations of unwanted items. The best thing about this, was that every now and then, Mum would bring home a bag, loaded with beautiful skirts, dresses, silk scarves and beads for Deb and me to dress up in. This was my idea of heaven!

Even back then as a youngster, I loved to feel girly, and I guess I've never really changed. I'm still the same now – long hair, with a penchant for floaty skirts and beaded jewellery. Mum, on the other hand, was the queen of jeans, t-shirts and trainers. In fact, I don't think she possessed anything else.

Mum's appearance didn't seem to bother her too much. Not that she ever looked untidy at all; just rather plain and practical. Plain and practical Sandra. And whereas I loved to be surrounded by objects of beauty, such things didn't seem important to Mum.

We ate our ice creams and skipped along the familiar pavement. "What time will Daddy be home?" I asked Mum. "We've started working on a wildlife project at school. Do you think I might see him tonight?"

"Daddy's come home early today, Judith," Mum replied. "We want to have a chat with you girls when we get back."

Dad was a long-distance lorry driver. He never came home early. How very strange, I thought. And stranger still that Mum never spoke another word all the way home.

* * *

He was waiting at the front door when we arrived back from school, a half-smile on his face. It wasn't his usual relaxed, open face. Dad looked different. Something in his eyes had changed. He knelt down and hugged us both; me first, and then Deb. "Come and sit down, girls," said Dad. "Your mother and I want to talk to you." He sat in the middle of our brown velour sofa, which had become somewhat saggy and threadbare over the years, and patted his hands down, gesturing for his beloveds to sit either side of him. We did so immediately, and Dad put his arms around us, pulling us close.

Mum took the armchair. Her face looked strained.

"Girls, there's no easy way of saying this..." she began. "Your father and I don't love each other any more. I've met a new partner and she's a woman. Her name is Francine, and Judith and I are going to go and live with her. She has a lovely big house in the country, and has a daughter called Suzette. Daddy is going to stay with Gran in Scotland until he finds a new house up there. Deborah, love, because you're starting senior school soon, you can choose whether you want to live down here with Judith and me, or go and live with Daddy in Scotland. You don't have to decide now. Just have a think about it."

And that was the day that my so-called 'normal' life (whatever that means) fell apart.

Being separated from Deb was alien and incredibly painful. She chose to begin a new life in Scotland with Dad and they had moved 500 miles away. Maybe she felt sorry for Dad, or maybe she couldn't bear the thought of living with a lesbian mother. I never really understood what led her to take that leap, but what I *did* know was that I missed them both terribly.

As soon as the school term was over, Mum and I moved in with Francine and her daughter, Suzette. Despite the strangeness of this new set up, I quickly grew fond of Francine. She was exceedingly beautiful and kind. In fact, her former career as a model was the reason behind her wealth and the amazing house

I was now living in. Though only ten minutes down the road, it was worlds apart from our old house which had been in desperate need of attention for several years.

Francine and I had lots in common. We were both arty and spiritually minded, both open to new experiences, and both loved to be surrounded by beautiful feminine things. Our love of floaty skirts, embroidered silks and colourful jewellery united us further. In fact, over the years, many people assumed that we were mother and daughter. Looking back, our similarities were uncanny; long hair, big eyes. Maybe that was what attracted Mum to Francine in the first place, an instant familiarity. Who knows; I never really asked.

They'd met through the charity that Mum had worked for. Francine was a regular donator, helping to fund the Macmillan shop. She had lost her mum to cancer several years before, and had recently undergone a lumpectomy herself. So being able to help this charity was of great personal importance.

The bond between her and Mum was incredibly intense, and now being older, I guess I can understand why they had to be together. But, my goodness, did I miss my dad…

In the years that followed, Dad had never wanted anyone else. Instead, he continued to hold a torch for Mum and saved every penny he had, in the hope that one day his precious family would once again be reunited. For the rest of my childhood, Dad became almost a fantasy figure of mine. I rarely got to see him, and deep down I think we probably both chased the same dream of being together again one day.

Deb came to stay during each school holiday, and it was heavenly to have her around. I know the feeling was mutual too, as we were virtually inseparable.

But life was very different when Deb wasn't there. Francine was lovely, and couldn't have been more welcoming, but her daughter Suzette was a completely different kettle of fish. Her dislike for me was instantly apparent, and for a long time I tried everything I could think of to please her.

Suzette was four years my senior, and as soon as she turned fourteen, our mums began to use her as a babysitter for me, enabling them to go out and have more quality time together. Suzette was always very keen to 'look after' me. In fact, she would offer her services quite frequently. Not only did it mean that she could earn some extra pocket money to spend on her penchant for heavy metal music, but it also gave her the perfect opportunity to carry out her fantasies, and abuse the annoying little kid that had invaded her home and bonded so nicely with her mother.

Just thinking about those times now makes me shudder…

* * *

Having just about managed the walk home from the tea shop, I opened the door to my flat and was instantly reminded of the mess I needed to attend to. Not having a dishwasher wasn't a problem when you washed up as you went along, but I'd let it build up, so now I'd just have to sort it out. Knowing I wouldn't relax until it was neat and tidy again, I lit an incense stick, popped the kettle on and filled the sink with bubbly water.

The actual act of washing up was never as bad as the thought of doing it was. I guess you can say that about most things really. Swishing your hands around in warm fragrant soapy bubbles was hardly a chore when you thought about it. I decided to embrace the moment, filling my cup on the side with boiling water. It wasn't my favourite mug, but was the only clean one, so it would suffice. My peppermint brew would be just the right temperature by the time I'd finished rinsing.

As I swirled the soapy sponge around the plate, I began to drift away again into past memories, thinking about Matt, rerunning the relationship through in my mind; trying to make sense of it all…

* * *

After our initial encounter, we were rarely apart. Either he was at my place, or I was at his. Rarely did I see the girls. I just wasn't bothered. Our frivolous girly nights out just couldn't compare to a night in with Matt. Besides, we were like magnets; two souls desperate to be united as one. Being apart just didn't feel right.

The intensity of our relationship continued, and we quickly moved in together, grabbing the opportunity to spend every moment possible in each other's company. I loved nothing more than cooking him wonderful, exotic meals; experimenting with new flavours and textures. To me, the process of cooking was all part of sharing my love with him. And my love-infused food always seemed to satisfy; heightening our senses and keeping life interesting. Even when we ate our meals we couldn't keep our hands off each other, somehow afraid to lose contact.

He would gently feed me, caressing me softly, teasing me with his sensual touch. And there was only ever one thing on the dessert menu. Making love with him was so deliciously sweet and satisfying. His touch, his smell, the way he felt against my skin. Why would I offer anything else?

Our love life was never dull. Our mutual creativity made sure of that, and I was willing to try anything to please him. Pleasing him in turn pleased me. And I realised that for the first time in years, I no longer craved my dad's love. I felt so complete with this man who seemed to give me everything I needed.

Not long after we'd moved in, Matt returned from work one evening with a concerned look on his face.

"Jude, can we sit down for a moment. There's something I need to say." With that, he took my hand, and led me towards our Moroccan-style day bed, sitting me down amongst the brightly coloured cushions. "Don't say anything, darling. Just listen will you?"

"Yes, of course," I replied, wondering what on earth was

coming next.

With that, he picked up his acoustic guitar and sat down, his body angled towards me. He handed me a scroll of parchment paper, tied up with a hessian string, and as I untied it, he began to sing the words that lay inside. It was his own version of the Beatles song, 'Hey Jude', which he'd written especially for me.

Matt's heartfelt serenade proclaimed that I was all he needed; that I'd taken his sad soul and made it better, and how becoming his wife would make him happy forever.

This declaration of eternal love so soon in our relationship took me completely by surprise; but it felt so right, and his words and sweetness filled my heart and touched the very core of my soul.

Then he got down on one knee, taking my hands in his. "Jude, my darling, you're everything I could wish for and more. My life would be meaningless if you weren't in it. Will you make me the happiest man alive and marry me?" With that, he removed a small box from his pocket and opened it in front of me to reveal a beautiful ring. Its three shades of gold were delicately entwined to encapsulate a heart-shaped, sparkly diamond.

This was the stuff of fairytales, I thought, and with tear-filled eyes, I took his face in my hands and kissed him tenderly. "Nothing would make me happier," I whispered, placing the ring on my finger and wrapping myself around him.

No further words were needed as we melted together in a symbolic union of joyous bliss.

Over the next few days, I set about painting him a picture of two turtle doves with their beaks tenderly touching, entitling it 'Mated for Life', and presenting it to him in a heart-shaped wooden frame. And that's what I truly believed; that we'd be together forever.

Within just a few months we were married. We opted for a ceremony which only he and I attended. Neither of us wanted or needed anyone else to be involved in our celebrations. It was just about the two of us; completely, entirely and absolutely.

We honeymooned in an amazing, character-filled, old and remote cottage in the Cotswolds, with only a few sheep for neighbours. And apart from visiting the nearest supermarket to stock up on food and wine, we hardly left each other's arms for the entire week. Who needed tropical climates when we had created our own heavenly paradise? Log fires, lavish rugs, a springy bed with crisp cotton sheets, and a bath plenty big enough for two, proved to be our perfect recipe for amusement, indulgence and sheer delight.

* * *

I put away the last of the saucepans, stacking it at precisely the right angle to fit in the tiny cupboard. I wiped down the worktop and picked up my peppermint tea, grabbing a pack of chocolate biscuits which would have to suffice for dinner. I hadn't the energy to even think about cooking anything. Leaving the bag in for maximum infusion, I took a few welcome sips, plonking myself down on the sofa with a sigh of relief. It felt good to take the weight off my ankle again, and I raised it up on the arm of the settee, adjusting it into a comfortable position, before switching on the TV.

With five minutes to spare before *Annie* started, I reached into the little pocket in my dress for my phone, thinking I'd just text Saffie quickly to see how Sol was feeling, and to let her know that everything was fine at the shop. As I lifted the phone, out flew the piece of paper with the lady's name and number neatly written on it. 'Annie'.

Annie. Now that was funny; a real coincidence, I thought. But something inside me somehow knew that if I could learn about positivity from little orphan Annie, then maybe I could learn something of even greater magnitude from the kind old lady in the tea room; whoever she was.

I popped Annie's details carefully into my jacket pocket. Maybe I *would* call her, just not tonight.

Chapter Three

I awoke with a jump, soon realising that I'd fallen asleep in front of the TV. It was two in the morning and my neck was stiff and painful. I peeled myself from the uncomfortable position on the sofa and stood up, quickly recalling that I'd been dreaming about Matt yet again. It was as if I could only make sense of it all by rerunning our relationship from start to finish over and over again until it finally sank in. So where was I? Yes, that's right; we had just got married...

* * *

A year later, Matt's job took him to India, and so without hesitation, I resigned from my job in a local department store, and accompanied him on a journey of adventure to that mind-blowing country.

It was an early afternoon in March when we touched down in Amritsar, Punjab, and we were met by a driver who was to take us to where Matt would be based.

"Mr and Mrs Richards? Welcome to India. My name is Arjan, and I will be taking you to your new home in Patiala. Allow me to take your cases. How was your flight?"

Matt looked relieved to relinquish responsibility of the trolley with the dodgy front wheel. "Thanks, Arjan. The flight was great."

Arjan held the car door open for me. "Your first time in India, Mrs Richards?"

"Yes! It's all very exciting, although I must admit, I'm rather nervous. My husband starts work tomorrow and I don't know anyone here, or anything about Punjab."

Arjan nodded and smiled at me kindly. "Please don't worry. We have everything covered."

Feeling slightly relieved, we relaxed into the comfortable seats and settled down for the journey.

Matt looked impressed. "Roads are good over here, Arjan. Not what I expected at all."

"Very good here in Punjab, sir. Patiala is excellent. You will have no problems getting around. Many places in India are not so good. We are very lucky."

"And it's not as hot as I imagined either," I added, closing my window and rubbing my bare arms. "I just assumed India would be roasting hot."

Arjan smiled at me in his rear-view mirror. "Our winter gets cold, Mrs Richards. But summer is on its way. Just you wait. It will get very hot indeed from next month."

I couldn't help wondering how he managed to tie his turban so neatly. A real art, I thought.

Matt placed his warm hand on my knee, sliding his little finger up between my thighs to give me a little tickle; ensuring his advances were out of Arjan's eye line. "We'll soon get you warmed up, my love, don't you worry."

The drive seemed to take forever, and all I could think about was being with my husband behind closed doors. We both had plenty of time to imagine the pleasure. For the rest of the journey, we teased each other subtly with looks, expressions and secret touch. It didn't matter where we were, so long as we were together.

As we arrived in Patiala, we were greeted by an array of colours, wonderful smells, and general liveliness. Arjan turned into a side street and pulled up at the kerb. "So, here we are. This is your apartment. Mr Richards, your colleague, Prakash Singh and his wife, Meeta will take you for dinner this evening at seven-thirty. Mrs Richards, Meeta will tell you all about Patiala and things to do while your husband is at work. You must not worry. She is very nice lady, like you."

He lifted our cases out of the boot. "Mr Richards, I hope you enjoy working here. Welcome to Patiala."

"Thanks, Arjan." Matt handed him a few notes, not really knowing their worth. Arjan nodded humbly and gestured with a wave.

The apartment looked like a holiday home; a basic cream building with black and gold gates on the front.

"This looks nice. Better than I expected."

"So long as the bed's comfy, we'll be fine," Matt grinned. "Shall we go and see?"

* * *

The doorbell rang, dead on seven-thirty. Not sure where we were going, I had opted for a simple shift-dress, jazzing it up with a statement necklace and a shawl.

"Hello, Matt. It's good to put a face to your voice at last. This is my wife Meeta."

Matt shook both of their hands warmly. "So good to see you, Prakash, and lovely to meet you, Meeta. This is my wife Jude."

Prakash seemed like an amiable chap, and Meeta had the warmest smile, making me feel very safe. Just what we needed, I thought.

"Meeta, I love your outfit, it's beautiful. I feel a bit casual. I hope this will be ok?"

"You look very beautiful, Jude, and what you wear is perfect. Welcome to Patiala."

We enjoyed a really pleasant couple of hours with our hosts. While the men talked mainly shop, Meeta seemed genuinely excited to show me around her city, and discover as much as she could about the UK.

Prakash arrived promptly again the following morning to collect Matt for work. He brought Meeta along with him, so I had no time to be lonely. A girly shopping day was on the cards, and I felt excited to seek out things that would make our simple apartment look really homely.

We made our way to a nearby bazaar, full of colourful silks and exotic spices. I couldn't help but feel totally alive there; my senses heightened by vibrant sounds and smells, not to mention the buzzing madness. Every stall looked like a shimmering rainbow of delight, be it offering food, fabric, shoes, beads or watches.

"This is Salwar Kameez," explained Meeta, pointing to an outfit like the one she had worn last night. "The Salwar is the trousers, and the Kameez is the tunic. Very typical Punjabi clothing for women. You want to try one? The blue is very nice for you."

"Why not," I replied, taking her suggested outfit behind the fabric curtain. The loose trousers felt really comfy, and the top fitted nicely, nipping me in at the waist. "Well? What do you think?"

"I think you are very beautiful in this, Jude. Please, allow me to buy this for you as a gift from Prakash and me." Leaving me no time to argue, or even respond, she paid the man, and before I knew it, we were heading deeper into the bazaar.

I bought some gorgeous silk cushions and a throw for our bed, and couldn't wait to surprise Matt with our new-look bedroom when he got home from work.

Meeta headed for the food stalls. "I must buy some vegetables for tonight."

"And I need to stock up our bare fridge, Meeta. The ingredients all look so wonderful and enchanting. Trouble is, I wouldn't have a clue what to do with most of them!"

Meeta smiled. "If you want to learn how to cook good Punjabi food, I introduce you to Gulab. She is a nice old lady who lives near you. Very good cook. Loves to share her knowledge. And her English is good enough that you will understand."

"That would be amazing. I'd really love that. Matt loves his food, and I love to cook for him. Thank you, Meeta."

"You're very welcome. I will call her later. She will be pleased. Now, let's get you some good tea, some bread, some fruit, some basmati, some nice pickles, and of course, some Chai Masala cake. Are you vegetarian?"

"No," I replied, wondering if I should be.

"We also get you some spiced chicken and some mutton then."

"Sounds great. That should keep us going." I smiled, feeling so relieved that this lovely lady was here with me, almost holding my hand. "You really are an angel."

"You're very welcome. It is nice for me too. Now, let me introduce you to the Punjabi street food. It is very delicious indeed, but stay away from that man's food over there, or you will get what you say is Delhi belly!" She chuckled.

"How come your English is so good?"

"I studied it at university. I wanted to get a job in the tourism industry, but when we married, we decided it's best that I stay at home." Meeta ordered three parathas, stuffed with spiced potatoes. "One each for us, and one for Matt tonight," she explained. "You can heat it up later for him."

We sat on a bench and enjoyed our lunch. The air was pleasantly warm, with a very light dry breeze. "All this lovely food is making me tired. Must be the jet lag kicking in."

"I take you home now, Jude. I need to prepare dinner for Prakash anyway, and I don't want him thinking I am just shopping all day," she winked. "I call Gulab later and let you know what she says."

We strolled back through the streets, Meeta helping me carry my heavy load, until we reached the familiar gates to my apartment. "However can I thank you?" I asked. "As soon as Gulab has worked her magic on me, I will cook for you and Prakash, I promise."

"That sounds very nice, Jude. I will look forward to it very much." Meeta smiled and waved as she trotted off to catch her bus home, her glossy black ponytail bouncing along behind her.

* * *

Hearing Matt's key turn in the door that evening, I stood in the hallway, wearing my new Punjabi outfit. I felt like a princess with all of the gold embroidery that edged my silk tunic. Matt dropped his case. "Wow! You look stunning, darling. Have you..."

I placed my finger over his lips. "I have a couple of things to show you but I'm not sure which to show you first. You can turn left into the kitchen where you will find stuffed parathas and fried chicken, or you can turn right to check out the new bedclothes I bought today at the bazaar."

"Suddenly, I don't feel all that hungry," Matt said, smiling. "Maybe the chicken can wait." He scooped me up and kicked open the bedroom door. "Let's have a look at these bedclothes then. And let me just make sure that it's still my Jude under all these fancy clothes." He unzipped my tunic. "Well, this gorgeous lady certainly looks like you. Let's see if she tastes like you, seeing as my appetite appears to be returning..."

When we finally emerged from the bedroom, Matt noticed a note lying on the doormat, addressed to me. It was a note from Meeta. I reddened at the possibility that we'd been too busy to hear her, or even worse, that she had heard our busyness, and I decided I'd better slip my robe around me, just in case.

Dear Jude,

I called Gulab and she is very happy to show you her cooking. Tomorrow she is making the atta for chapattis and parathas. If you want to go, she will see you at 10am.

Walk out of your street, turn left on to the main road and she is only a few houses down. Number 303. If you make her a donation, she will give you some atta to take home.

I see you soon. Good sleep.
Meeta

What a sweetie she was.

"This bread is delicious, darling."

"Hopefully I'll be able to make it for you myself soon, babe," I said, massaging his shoulders. "Meeta has arranged some cookery lessons for me. There's a lady nearby who seems happy to teach me what to do with all the local ingredients and wonderful spices."

Putting his plate down, Matt took my hands and twisted me round so I was facing him, sliding his hands into my robe. "Stunningly gorgeous, great in bed, *and* a good cook, eh? I must be the luckiest man alive."

"You say all the right things, darling. Anyway, how was your day? Are the people nice?"

"It was good thanks. Well, up until I got home it was good, and then my day got even better." He kissed me, pulling me close. "In a nutshell, it was great and I felt very welcome. But right now I feel ever so tired, so how about we have an early night, and save the talking till tomorrow? I seem to remember liking those new bedclothes you bought."

Chapter Four

It was no use. Sleep wasn't happening, so I dragged myself up from my lonely bed and threw my dress into the washing basket. I carefully removed my thick tights, cautiously peeling them away from the sore, throbbing and weepy scab that lay hidden beneath. I stepped into the shower, hoping to find some comfort in my favourite rose-scented wash. There was something wonderful about the smell of rose that somehow soothed my soul, albeit temporarily.

I dressed my ankle with a piece of gauze and opted for some full-length leggings to mask the wound. With no appetite for breakfast, I took extra time to somehow disguise how rough I felt, applying plenty of cooling eye gel and extra blusher on the apples of my cheeks. With any luck, my customers wouldn't suspect a thing today, and maybe Saffie would still be at home with Sol.

But then again, perhaps not. "Blimey, Jude, are you ok? You look dreadful!"

"Hi, Saff. Bad night. Same old, same old. Just can't seem to move forward. It's like I'm caught in Matt's web and there's no way out. Anyway, enough about that; I'm sick to the back teeth of it all. How's Sol?" I flicked the kettle on in the back room of the shop and tipped several teaspoons-worth of coffee into my mug, hoping it would somehow inject some life into me.

"He's on the mend thanks, Jude. Gone back into school today. I've said he can come home for lunch though, so I'll be out for a while later." She turned to me, concern etched across her face. "What are we going to do with you, my love? You can't go on feeling like this. What you need is a reading to give you some clarity and direction; something positive to focus on. I used to know a lady who was very good, but she moved away."

"I'll take any help I can get, Saff. I just need an end to this torture. I so want to move on, but I haven't a clue how. I hate to admit it, and I know I'm an idiot, but I still love him." I held up the coffee and tea canisters.

"That selfish bastard doesn't deserve your love, Jude. God forbid, if I ever saw him, I'd swing for him. I'll have a coffee too please, darling."

We sipped our coffees, deep in thought, almost forgetting to turn the shop sign to OPEN! The morning looked to be pretty uneventful, so rather than run the risk of nodding off at the counter, I decided to go out the back and keep busy with a stock check. That way, I couldn't scare any customers away with my ghostly appearance; Halloween had already been and gone after all.

"I'm off now, Jude, my love. I'll see you later."

I poked my head out to reply, but Saffie was already out of earshot, and I noticed that a woman had walked in through the door. She looked interesting; her thick hair piled up high with a sharp fringe that framed her piercingly icy eyes, heavy with black liner. A gap in her long velvet coat revealed a host of silver necklaces of differing lengths, each supporting magical charms; a pentacle, crystal pendants and a fairy. They clinked and clattered with every movement, becoming louder as she approached.

"Hello, dear. I wonder if you'd be kind enough to display some business cards for me? I work locally from home as a psychic medium and I really love helping people to move forward with their lives. I thought your shop looked like the right sort of place to advertise. In fact, if you wouldn't mind putting one of these posters in your window, I'd be very happy to give you a free reading in exchange."

She held out a bundle of cards and I noticed that her name was Rose. Then I noticed that my mouth was hanging open in disbelief, and wondered what Rose must have thought of me. Somewhat curious and flabbergasted by the timing of this happening, and swiftly closing my mouth again, I gratefully accepted her offer and arranged to visit her home on Friday evening.

Was it my imagination, or had a lady named after my favourite flower that soothed my soul, just agreed to help shine some light on my dark and dismal situation?

With a secret hope in my heart and growing excitement in my belly, I pinned Rose's poster in the window. Friday, which was only two days away, couldn't come soon enough. Maybe today wasn't so bad after all, and I eagerly anticipated Saffie's return so I could tell her all about my bizarre encounter. I hadn't felt this excited and nervous since our adventures in Punjab.

* * *

I went to knock at the door of no. 303, but it was already open, so I poked my head tentatively round, to find a jolly round face looking back at me. "Come in, come in!"

"Oh, hello, and thank you. I'm Jude. Are you Gulab?"

"Yes, yes, come in. We make atta. I show you." Her apron was covered in flour, and she offered me a stool at the worktop. "First I show you atta. Then we have chai." She smiled warmly.

"I brought some paper and a pen with me. I hope you don't mind if I make notes as we go along?"

"Ok, no problem. So, first we take two cups of flour in bowl, then we put half spoon salt and mixing together. Now we put four spoons oil and mixing all together. Next we put this much warm water in bowl and mixing it all up. And put more warm water and mixing, and more water and mixing and when its good like this, no more water. Good atta. Now we knead atta. Keep like this, kneading. Kneading, kneading, kneading. Punjabi ladies strong arms! Now, when good atta like this, we leave it and make chai! You are English, you like chai yes?"

"Oh, yes please. I'd love a cup of tea." We sipped our tea

together while the dough was left to stand. "Thank you so much for showing me your wonderful cooking, Gulab. I can't wait to make your food for my husband."

"You come again next week?' she asked. "We make Dal Makhani. Very good."

"If that's ok with you, then I'd love to."

"Good. I tell you what you need. You take this to bazaar and you bring here next time." She handed me a list of ingredients, none of which I could understand.

"Ok, atta is ready now, so we make the balls for the golf like this and dip them in flour. Now we roll like this and make oil very hot in pan. Now we fry like this, turning, turning, turning. Then we have good chapatti. If you don't wanting all the atta, you can put in here or here," she explained, pointing to the fridge and the freezer.

"Now we have chapatti, we can eat like this for the breakfast." Gulab rolled her chapatti and dipped it in her tea. "Or we can make it with good things inside. Vegetables, spices. I show you." She proceeded to demonstrate the making of stuffed parathas with cauliflower and also with potatoes. I watched carefully, noting everything down and admiring this lady's passionate work of art.

For several weeks through the Punjabi summer, I visited Gulab, collecting the correct ingredients early from the market on the way to her, before it got too hot. She always seemed so pleased to share her skills with me. Despite the intense heat, we enjoyed each other's company, and by the time June came, I had mastered Mutton Biryani, Tandoori Chicken, Dal Makhani, Poori bread, Chai Masala cake, and several variations of Lassi, a yoghurt-based drink which was great for breakfast.

It didn't take me long to settle into our Punjabi life. I quickly learnt from Meeta and other local Indian ladies about their amazing beauty routines, and spent an hour each day, nourishing, pampering and preening myself to please my man.

"Always make the last rinse with vinegar." One lady told me, looking at my hair. "And you must rub lemon juice over your hands before washing them to keep them young." I took all of these tips on board.

So most mornings I would head to the bazaars, collecting silks, cushions and ornaments for the home, and fresh ingredients for our evening meal. Life was good, and Matt and I were happy. Still in love, and still excited by each other.

And every Friday, I would go along to the Punjabi University of Patiala; an imposing white building that looked like a giant stormtrooper, and attend a kundalini yoga class with Meeta. She was such a kind soul. Always at the end of the phone when I needed her; a truly precious friend.

But it was the early hours of one Saturday morning, when we received a call from my big sister Deb, that would change things forever.

Matt passed me the phone. "Hello? Deb? Are you ok?" I hadn't heard from her in months.

"Jude, it's Dad. He's not good. He's been struggling for breath the last couple of weeks. We thought it was an allergy or something, but things got really bad last night and we had to call for an ambulance." Her voice was strained. "He's having to wear an oxygen mask to breathe."

I sat bolt upright, feeling fully awake. "What's wrong with him, Deb? Is he going to be ok?"

"They've run lots of tests today and his consultant's pretty sure it's a lung disease. If he's right, then he won't recover."

"What?"

"He's asked to see you, Jude. He's stable at the moment, but he needs you with him."

Without too much thought, I told Deb that I would get to her as soon as I could. I just had to be there for my beloved Dad, and neither hell nor high water could have stopped me. The thought of him suffering churned my insides. How dreadful not to be able to breathe. When I tried to contemplate his life on earth being over, my head felt as though it would explode. It just didn't bear thinking about, so I tried to put this to the back of my mind as I planned my journey home and booked my flights.

Matt seemed pretty quiet. He only had two months left out here, so we agreed that he would stay until the end of his contract before returning home. The thought of us being apart for that long filled me with dread – not being able to look after him or make a fuss. But I had no choice. This might be the last chance I got to see my Dad. Even still, I could tell he wasn't happy to be left alone. So when he took his shower that evening, I wrote a little poem to remind Matt of how much I loved him.

Still a little dazed at the day's news, I took a long, hot shower, and we shared what was to be our last meal together in India. Our lovemaking was deeply passionate that night, and as we lay there, our bodies entwined, we promised each other that we'd start trying for a family on Matt's return. The thought of this filled me with hope, and gave us both something special to hang on to.

The following morning, our parting was painful and intense. I could tell that Matt didn't want me to go, but despite his reluctance, I jumped on the first flight out of Punjab, and embarked upon what seemed like the longest journey in history, back to Dad's house in Scotland. I hadn't a clue how long I'd be staying there, but I hoped it would be for long enough to say all the things I wanted to say to my dear dad.

Chapter Five

"What are you still doing here, Judith?" Saffie asked, her hands resting mockingly on her hips. "I thought you were leaving early today. You haven't forgotten about your reading tonight have you?"

"To be honest, Saff, it's the only thing that's kept me going since Wednesday. I'll be off then, if you're sure you don't mind."

"Mind? You've done me enough favours lately, Jude. I hope you get whatever you need from it, my love. Ask her if she's got a magic smile potion for you will you? And save me a drop if she has." She winked. "Let me know how you get on!"

"Will do! See you tomorrow, Saff." We hugged and I headed off home.

I'd felt lifted by Rose's kind offer of a reading, but was now feeling incredibly nervous. I'd enjoyed a palm reading from a woman in a Punjabi market once, which was more for fun, but I'd never sought out a psychic to help me with my life difficulties. What would she say, I wondered? What could she tell? Would she be able to explain how I went from being totally happy to losing it all and ending up in this dark and painful place?

I made myself a cuppa, and plonked my weary bones down on the sofa for a quick rest before I headed out to Rose's place. Above all else, I hoped this reading would bring me closer to Dad. That way I wouldn't feel quite so alone. I thought back to my return from India to Scotland...

* * *

In spite of my exhaustion from the long flight, I was unable to rest, and spent the next few hours busying myself on nervous energy, texting Matt to let him know I was safe, and buying a card and a few groceries to lift Dad's spirits.

I arrived promptly that evening for visiting time, and the clinical smell of the hospital churned my already-anxious stomach as I followed the signs to Dad's ward. Fortunately, his bed was the first one I came to, and the whole of me felt this overwhelming sense of relief when I saw his face again. I kissed his head and held his hand, determined not to show him any of my anguish. The last thing he needed was to worry about my upsets.

Frustrated by not having the breath to converse at length with me, his baby girl, Dad rested his head back on his pillow, and listened to my tales of India, and how my wonderful husband and I were planning on starting a family as soon as he returned. I so wanted Dad to know that I was secure, settled and happy, believing that it really meant the world to him.

As the bell rang to mark the end of visiting time, our hearts sank as we said goodbye, both trying to hide our disappointed sadness that we once again had to be parted. Kissing Dad's forehead to avoid his oxygen mask, I promised to return tomorrow afternoon, and put on my best smile as I walked away. But the moment the ward door closed behind me, I cried and cried all the way home, until there were no tears left in me.

I waited until 11.30pm before calling Matt to update him on my dreadful experience. It was early morning in India, and he'd be stirring by then.

My husband listened lovingly to my tearful recollection of the hospital visit. "It'll be ok," he reassured me through my sorrow. "I'm here for you, baby. You'll always have me to lean on you know. I've got broad shoulders for a reason. I love you, darling, and I miss you so much, but we'll be together again soon, and I'll make it all better for you, I promise. I'll kiss all of your pain away."

His loving words were just what I needed, and I felt secure knowing that I could depend on this gorgeous man to protect me and keep me safe. If only he was here with me.

The weeks that followed seemed like one long living nightmare. I tried to keep myself busy in an attempt to numb the anxiety I felt when I wasn't with Dad. The arrival of visiting times seemed to take forever, and knowing that my lovely dad was all alone, struggling to breathe, totally dependant on the busy nurses, was incredibly distressing.

Just to see his face brighten was a huge relief, as was the notion of us being together for a little while longer. But that feeling was short-lived, and all too soon the dreaded bell would ring again, wrenching me away once more.

Deb rarely visited, which I found hard to understand. After all, she'd lived with Dad and they'd always been close; a closeness that I had craved. She didn't seem to want to share in this difficult time with me, which was painful. A few throwaway comments led me to suspect that she was jealous of Dad's love for me, but maybe this was her way of dealing with the inevitable loss of our father.

I needed Matt's love more than ever. I felt vulnerable and missed him dreadfully. The thought of his return, and the hope of us creating a child together, was all that was keeping me going. I couldn't wait to have his body next to mine again – strong, warm and protective. It was as though a big part of me was missing.

Three and a half weeks had passed since I'd made the journey from India to Scotland and I was now, both emotionally and physically exhausted.

Wondering whether each passing day would be the last time I'd see my dad, I dared not miss a day's visiting. Quite often, I'd go twice, ensuring he wouldn't spend too much time on his own. Although seeing his face and being beside him brought me great reassurance, I also watched him grow weaker and weaker, struggling to catch his breath, and finding it increasingly impossible to speak. The comforting thing was that we'd had some lovely, meaningful conversations in our first few days, so it felt like nothing important had been left unsaid. Just being there and holding his hand was exactly what he needed, and exactly what I needed too. To think that I'd dreamt of being this close to my daddy again for all these years… What I hadn't envisaged though, was how much pain and sadness would accompany the closeness.

I missed Matt terribly, and as the weeks went by, I felt increasingly needy of his love and support to help me refuel somehow. But at the same time, I felt weighted down with guilt that I couldn't be with him, and was therefore unable to give him what he was used to – my undivided attention and our physical closeness.

Matt's phone calls became less frequent, and it became apparent that whenever I called him, he was limited on time due to work pressures. His tone was now rarely soft or loving, and I sensed that he was cross with me for putting my energy elsewhere and not fully into our relationship. He hadn't said anything along these lines; it was just a feeling. He hadn't, come to think of it, said much at all. On the other hand, however, perhaps I was imagining it – I was incredibly tired and drained after all. Nevertheless, it frightened me to feel this needy of someone – to feel that my emotional stability was dependant on his words and tone. After all, he'd promised to be my rock, to be my protector and to kiss all of the hurt away.

My whole being ached for him. Maybe if I hadn't left him behind… Maybe if I tried a bit harder to think of how he must be feeling… Maybe it would all be different when I was in his arms again and we began to plan our family… Maybe…

* * *

The memories were too much to bear and I grasped a bunch of hair from the nape of my neck, ripping it out from its roots. The sudden intensity of the pain brought me instantly back into the here and now. I looked up at the clock and realised it was time to leave for Rose's. I quickly grabbed some painkillers on the way out, and a biscuit to prevent any tummy grumblings. I arrived at the address I'd been given, to find a tiny but pretty little cottage. The darkness of the evening made it a little spooky, but perhaps that was just my imagination running away with me again. 'Rose Cottage' was dimly lit and I made my way to the front door, tapping gently on the knocker. Rose greeted me with a warm smile and I felt instantly reassured that I was safe.

She led me up a spiral staircase, her heeled boots hanging over the back of each stair as she ascended, and her silver jewellery tinkling with every movement.

"Ever had a reading before, dear?"

"Only a palm reading in India. Life seemed good then so it was only for a bit of fun. But you won't believe how timely your kind offer was. I could certainly do with a bit of guidance."

"Oh, I believe it alright. There's no such thing as a coincidence you know."

Rose offered me a chair, and we sat down at a small round table, covered in a crushed velvet red cloth. A single pink rose in a tiny vase, a lit candle, and a sparkling lump of pale blue crystal had been carefully placed, allowing plenty of room for a well-used deck of cards which sat in the middle, face down.

"Beautiful rose. Is it scented?"

"It's from the garden, dear, and yes, it smells divine." She held the rose towards my nose.

"There's something very comforting about the smell of roses. They really are my favourite."

"Mine too." Rose smiled. "Now, don't think I'm being rude, dear, but I need you to sit quietly for me for a few minutes while I tune in to what's going on."

We sat together in the candle-lit room, my stomach doing summersaults with the anticipation of it all.

"Ok, dear. I'm seeing a kilt, so I'm feeling the presence of a Scottish male and I'm pretty sure he's in the spirit world. He is showing me two lights and I'm wondering if this is representing either his children or grandchildren. Whoever they are, they are very precious to him. Does that mean anything to you?"

"Yes, it does," I replied, not wanting to give too much away. I felt relieved and comforted to know that Dad was with me.

"No one else seems to be coming forward at the moment, dear, so let's ask the Scottish man to stay with us while I shuffle the cards. Now, as it's guidance that you need, let's get a bit more insight into the problem itself." She began to lay some cards face down in what seemed to be an ordered spread.

"First, we have the three of swords so I'm instantly being shown heartbreak – the worst pain of all. I'm getting huge internal conflict, dear, so I'm guessing things seem very difficult for you at the moment."

I nodded, hoping Rose wouldn't notice the tears beginning to well up. She reached across to the windowsill and grabbed a few tissues from a pretty box, passing them to me. "Tears are healing you know. Don't be afraid to let them come." The nape of my neck pulsated with pain.

"Now then, let's understand what this pain is all about." She turned the next card. It was the Devil. She nodded knowingly to herself. "As I thought, and as harsh as it may sound, it appears that you have been dancing to the Devil's tune. Let's look at this card together. You see, the Devil here represents the dark side of life, and of you. He is the opposite of love. He is fear, he is neediness, he is addiction, and he can be very powerful – but only if you let him. Now, this little puppet here is being operated by the Devil. It is doing whatever the Devil wants. It thinks it has to. It thinks it can't survive without him. The truth is though, that it can break free from the chains at any point if it chooses to turn to the light. So this card is telling you not to be afraid, but to turn away from your fears and answer only to love. Now you must ask yourself, is this addictive substance or person feeding me with love? Am I feeling good about myself when I'm with this person or substance? Does that make sense, dear?"

"It makes perfect sense, Rose. But what if you don't know how to free yourself?"

"Let's look to the cards for insight." She turned the next card. "Ok, we have the Ten of Swords. Now this figure here is you, lying down with ten swords in your back. Not literally, but metaphorically. Things look pretty grim. But you can see in the distance that things are starting to improve. The sky is clearing and the horizon looks bright. And so we conclude that this represents the ending of a difficult time, clearing the way for new beginnings. Although this card looks pretty painful, it is actually very positive. You won't have to suffer like this for too much longer, dear."

Rose turned over the next card. "Right then, this is the person that will help you move forward; the Queen of Cups. She is emotionally mature and highly intuitive. I am getting the sense of a large presence, bold and bright. Our Scottish man is showing me a very bright lipstick. And if you haven't already met this lady, you soon will."

I felt shocked. Could this be that lady from the coffee shop – Annie? It had to be. This was all a little bit spooky.

"Right, so we know that someone will help you, but what do you need to do to allow the healing to begin?" She turned the penultimate card over on the table. "The Ace of Cups. You need to open your heart to love and to the Divine guidance that surrounds you every day. You need to get out of your head and move forward from the heart. Ask for guidance and have faith that you will receive it. Scottish man seems very keen to help you too!" Rose chuckled.

The tears had stopped now and I breathed a large sigh. I felt hopeful that things actually might start to get better. There was one card remaining on the table.

"So let's see what will be the outcome if you follow this guidance then, dear." Rose turned over the card. "Lovely. The

Queen of Pentacles. She is our Earth Mother and she represents those qualities in you; loving and wise; in perfect tune with nature and the cycles of life. She nurtures both herself and others. She loves her body and looks after her health. She accepts what she cannot change and she goes with the flow. This really is ever so positive and a lovely card to finish on. Now then, dear, is there anything else you want to ask while you're here?"

I cleared my throat. "Will I ever have a successful relationship that doesn't end in pain?"

Rose smiled. "Well, the Queen of Pentacles tells us that we must first learn to love ourselves." She picked another card and placed it in the centre of the spread. "The Two of Cups. A beautiful card, and very telling too. This represents a meeting of hearts. A stable relationship on equal footings. It is a deep love that is based around friendship and mutual respect. So it would seem, dear, that once you've turned this corner, your future will be very bright indeed! Our Scotsman is showing me a swan. Does that mean anything to you?"

"Not really," I replied, deeply wishing I knew what it meant.

"Well, not to worry. Just hold it in your mind and I'm sure it will become clear when the time is right." Rose gathered up her cards and shuffled them back into the pack. "Now, would you like a glass of water before you head off, or do you feel ok?"

"I'm fine thank you, Rose. Thanks so much. You won't believe how appropriate the cards have been. It's really helped."

Rose chuckled. "My pleasure, dear. The cards are always appropriate, believe me. Now, so long as you feel ok, that just leaves us to say thank you to any guides that have assisted us with our reading, especially our Scottish man."

"Thanks, Dad," I added, and Rose smiled. She saw me to the front door and told me that the next bus would be here any minute.

"I loved your cards, Rose. Where can I get a deck?"

"They're lovely, aren't they? I'll pick up a pack for you and bring them into the shop. Now get on your way or you'll miss your bus."

I trotted down her driveway towards the bus stop, and despite the darkness beyond, I felt lighter than I had in a long time. Maybe things were looking up already.

Chapter Six

It was Saturday morning and I'd got to work earlier than usual, arriving before Saff.

"Blimey! You're a bit eager! What are you doing standing there? Waiting to roll the red carpet out for me?" Saffie winked. The wind had played havoc with her hair and she attempted to smooth it back down with her hands.

"Must've left my keys in the shop yesterday. Honestly, my brain at the moment…"

She unlocked the door, keeping one eye on me the whole time. "Well? How did it go? Give me detail. Omit nothing!"

"It was excellent thanks, Saff; very reassuring. Rose reckons that once I've turned this corner, the future will be very bright."

"Well, that's good to hear. About time you got a break. Coffee?"

"Ooh, yes please."

She filled our mugs and reached for the milk. "So? What else did she say?"

"Well, I'm certain that my dad came through right at the beginning, which felt amazing. I've missed him so much, Saff."

"No need to miss him if he's with you, honey."

"Yeah, I'm kinda feeling that now. Anyway, the cards were spot on. The heartbreak, the getting stabbed in the back; it all rang true. And then she said I'd been dancing to the Devil's tune."

"The Devil being shit-face bastard Matt, I take it?"

"He's still my husband you know, Saff."

"Husband? That spineless arsehole offered you not one bit of support through your dad's illness."

"But I *did* leave him out in India. Anyway, he came back for the funeral. That must count for something."

"Yes, and while he was back he slept with your sister too. On your thirtieth birthday of all occasions. Or have you forgotten that bit?"

"Of course I haven't forgotten. Look, I know you hate him, and I wish I could hate him too, but my heart still aches for him, Saff, and a part of me still wishes he'd call so we can put things right. I know it sounds stupid, but you can't help who you fall in love with."

"No, but you can learn about self-respect. I'm sorry, Jude, I know I sound harsh, but it's only coz I love you, and sometimes I think you need to hear the truth, even though it hurts." Saff put her arms around me and rubbed my shoulders. She lifted my chin up so that our eyes met. "So come on then, back to this reading. What else did she say?"

"She said I need to free myself from the chains that bind, and that a tall, intuitive lady would help me."

"Well, that rules short-arse-me out then!"

I couldn't help but laugh. "I think I know who Rose meant, Saff. I think I've met her already. Anyway, she said that if I learn to love and nurture myself, then I will find love again. Whether that love is Matt or not, I don't know."

"Not if you love yourself it won't be." I knew Saffie meant well, and that she had my best interests at heart. I just wished my outlook was as clear and simple as hers seemed to be. She'd had her fair share of heartache too. Her husband left her for a younger model when she was heavily pregnant with Sol, so I couldn't blame her for being a bit anti-men.

A supplier came in to chat to Saffie, followed by a steady flow of customers. Rarely were we rushed off our feet, but we could pretty much guarantee a higher level of activity on Saturdays. The day passed quickly, and before I knew it, I was home again.

I knew what I had to do. I reached for my jacket, removing the slip of paper from its inside pocket. Although I'd done nothing with it in the week that had passed, it had felt comforting to know it was there. And since my reading with Rose last night, I was sure that it was going to be useful.

Tentatively, and with shaky hands, I dialled the number. But as soon as I heard it ring, I quickly hung up. What on earth would I say anyway? Where would I begin? I made myself a cup of tea, feeling disappointed and disheartened by my lack of courage. *People appear in your life for a reason,* I thought, *and this woman appeared out of nowhere, tapped into my feelings, and offered me support.*

I finished my tea, and summoned the nerve to redial.

"Hello, Annie speaking." Her voice was low and authoritative, yet friendly. Not quite knowing how to start this conversation, or indeed, even if she'd remember me, I nervously began to speak.

"Oh, hello, Annie. My name's Jude. We sort of met in the coffee shop last week. You probably don't remember, but you kindly gave me your number and…"

"Hello, darling. I'm glad you phoned," she replied. "I've been waiting for you."

Without much encouragement, I proceeded to tell Annie about pretty much everything. Not in detail, but I explained about the pain and anguish of watching Dad suffocate to his death and how helpless that made me feel. I told her about Deb withdrawing from me when Dad got ill, and leaving almost all of the hospital visits to me. I explained that Matt's contract had got extended in Punjab and how much I missed him, despite his betrayal with my sister. And I told her that I was self-harming again and didn't know how to stop.

Annie listened, "mmm-ing" every now and again as if she was nodding. Not once did she say "that's awful" or "poor you". Her tone remained calm as if she wasn't at all surprised.

"Well, I'm sorry you've had such a difficult time, darling, but I think I may be able to help if you'll allow me to."

"Yes please, Annie, I'm open to anything. I know I can't go on like this."

"Right then. I've been setting up a group. Well, a programme really, to help people who are struggling, with their recovery. The first session starts this Wednesday evening at seven-thirty, in the small room at the back of the village hall. If you'd like to join us then all you need to bring is a small donation to help towards the room hire and refreshments. That *and* an open heart if you can. Now, how does that sound?"

"It sounds wonderful. Thank you so much, Annie. I'll see you then."

"Right oh, darling. Any problem meantime, you know where I am," she said in the same calm tone before hanging up.

Chapter Seven

I snapped my umbrella shut, opening and closing it a few times more to shake off the excess rain. The hall looked a bit dingy from the outside and I hoped the inside was a tad more welcoming. I took off my jacket and popped my umbrella down in the corner, next to a couple of other ones. The entrance smelt rather musty. Not unpleasant as such; just not aired sufficiently. My stomach was doing summersaults. I'd been seriously nervous all day and had been far too anxious to eat. This really was unknown territory.

As I walked into the main room, I saw a circle of chairs, most of which had already been filled. But wait. Where was Annie? Not wanting to cause a fuss, I sat down in one of the three vacant chairs. No one was talking to each other and most people nodded at me before looking back down at the floor.

"Alright?" said the bloke sitting next to me with a wink and a semi-smile.

"Hello," I replied politely. He looked like a throwback from the eighties. Tight stonewashed jeans, a white 'muscle' top with a V-neck that revealed plenty of chest hair, a matching chunky neck chain and bracelet in muted gold, and a shoulder-length head of shaggy, highlighted hair, pulled loosely back in a ponytail. I popped my bag down on the floor, noticing his deck-shoes which housed his hairy feet. There was no doubt about it; this bloke was furry. I joined the others in their awkward attempts to avoid eye contact, secretly wondering how this man's jewellery didn't get caught up in his shag-piled pecs.

I heard a toilet flush and Annie appeared from the ladies', walking confidently to her seat, acknowledging everyone with a friendly smile. She was as I remembered; tall and solidly built, with steel grey hair. She wore a vibrant raspberry pink jumper with lipstick to match, and a large blue ring made of lapis lazuli.

It was hard to tell her age, but I reckoned she was in her late seventies, or maybe even a healthy-looking eighty.

She looked at her watch. It was seven-thirty-five.

"Ok, darlings, I'm just waiting for one more, so let's give them a couple of minutes' grace, seeing as it's their first time. After that, folks, if you don't show up on time, you'll still be very welcome to join us, but we *will* start without you." She grinned a cheeky smile that seemed to put everyone in the room at ease.

Annie busied herself by putting some papers in order and reading an excerpt from a well-fingered book.

"Ok, darlings, let's make a start. It's a shame that we have one seat still empty but that's obviously how it's meant to be this time, so let's just accept it. Right then. Let's begin by introducing ourselves. As we go round, I'd like each individual to say their name, and then for the rest of the group to repeat the name back to them. If we can start with you then please."

Annie gestured to a timid-looking lady to her left, dressed in a pale pink twinset and a grey A-lined skirt. What with her short mousey hair and pale complexion, she looked as though she would quite like to fade into the uninteresting wallpaper behind her. As she opened her mouth to speak, her cheeks twitched nervously. "Hello, I'm Martha."

"Martha," we all replied, awkwardly. Mousey Martha, I thought. I was terrible at remembering names, so had a habit of creating my own versions so they would stick. I never meant it unkindly. It just helped, that's all.

We moved our gaze to the next person in line; a friendly-looking chubby gent with dark grey hair and a black moustache. "Pleased to meet you all. I'm Ray."

"Ray," we chanted back. The Great Raymondo, I thought.

The introductions continued around the circle, getting closer and closer to me, and as we reached the hairy chap next to me, my stomach flipped madly and I felt my throat redden. I wasn't used to speaking in front of people.

"Hi, guys, I'm Shane." Oh yes, Shane the Mane. That one would certainly stick.

Oh, God, it was my turn now. "Hi, I'm Jude."

"Jude," everyone responded. It felt really good to be acknowledged by the group, and I now understood Annie's suggestion. It eased the loneliness somehow.

"And I'm Annie."

"Annie," we all replied, smiling.

"So, darlings, welcome, and thank you for being here, at what I hope will be the first meeting of many. Before we begin, I have a few rules that I believe are very important for us all to adhere to. First of all, we are all equal. Just because I'm sitting here leading this evening's meeting, doesn't mean that I am any better than you, and you all have as much right to speak and be heard as anyone else in this group. Secondly, what is said in the room stays in the room. This must remain a safe place where we can explore and share our innermost thoughts and feelings, and so out of this room, we must practise and respect complete anonymity. Is that understood?" Everyone nodded in agreement.

"Now, the aim of this group is to provide a place where we can come together and support each other through difficult times, using a recovery programme that applies to us all. So who am I to have done this? Well, over twenty years ago, I set up an Al-Anon group that is still going strong to this day. And as some of you may know, Al-Anon is an organisation that offers a recovery programme to the loved ones of alcoholics. My lovely late husband had a real problem with drink, God bless him.

"Now, whether alcohol does or doesn't feature in your own life problems, matters not. I strongly believe that we all need a recovery programme that will restore us to sanity when times get tough. Because let's face it, life does not always appear to be a bed of roses does it? And that's why we're all sitting here this evening. We all need some support and guidance at some point or another. And for us, that point is now.

"Now then, darlings, I must share a little secret. So the saying goes, *with age, comes wisdom*. And there's no doubt about it – I am extremely old! And hopefully wise too. And I have felt guided, not only to set up this group, but also to approach and speak with each of you, and I must trust in these feelings. I truly believe that together, with total love and commitment, we can move mountains."

Annie peered at her watch again. "Well, time is of the essence, and there's only so much we can cover in each session, so please bear with and be patient. Everyone will have ample opportunity to share their concerns, but it can't all happen tonight.'

She turned to face me. "Well, Jude, dear, I can't keep going clockwise around the room so let's start with you if we may. Do you feel up to telling the group why you are here and what kind of support you'd like from the others?"

Not wanting to be rude to Annie, I nodded and took a deep breath. "Ok then. Crikey, I'm not sure where to start."

Annie smiled sympathetically "How about at the beginning? Take your time. You'll be fine."

"Errmm, ok then. Well, I guess my life began to get difficult when my parents divorced and I was separated from my dad and my sister, both of whom I was very close to. They lived together, and I lived with my mum, her new female partner Francine, who was always lovely to me, and her daughter Suzette, who was not. Suzette was several years older than me and so was often left to look after me when Mum and Francine went out. She was always perfectly charming to me in front of them, but as soon as we were alone, she would say the most awful things.

"Typical things were that I was ugly and stupid, that no one liked me, that our mums wished I'd gone to live with my dad instead. But the weird thing was, she would always say these things with a smile on her face. She would make me a drink and tell me she'd put bleach in it. And she would say cruel things about my mum's appearance, knowing that I'd never hurt my mum by repeating what she said.

"I ended up feeling so bad about myself – ugly, guilty, worthless and alone. I missed my dad and I didn't know where to turn. I was convinced I was an awful person and it was then that I began to pull my hair out. Causing myself pain helped me to momentarily forget my feelings. It was a release; a bit like crying I guess, but without the tears.

"This went on for years, progressing from pulling my hair out, to burning myself, to making myself bleed. But this all stopped when I met my husband Matt."

I felt the tears starting to well again, and I swallowed hard to clear the lump of tension from my throat. "We were so happy together, like soul mates. I felt so loved. He was all I needed. We got married, moved to India with his work and everything was wonderful. We were planning on starting a family…"

The tears were rolling down my cheeks now, burning as they went.

"Then I found out my dad was ill and I flew back. My sister became distant, and it felt like she wanted to hurt me. And then Matt became distant, and it felt like he wanted to hurt me too. My dad died two weeks before my thirtieth birthday, and Matt flew back for the funeral. We were staying with my sister at my dad's house in Scotland, and Matt suggested I go for a pamper day at the local spa. He'd bought me two treatments and lunch there as a birthday treat. But during my massage, I got really upset and decided to go home early. I just wanted Matt to hold me. But as I walked through the door, I heard a commotion. Both he and Deb were naked. They'd been enjoying a day of passion while I was out of the way. Turned out that, unbeknown to me, they'd been texting each other for weeks.

"Matt was furious, saying that it was all my fault for abandoning our relationship; for not showing him enough love, and then he flew back to India where, as far as I know, he still is.

"So I'm now renting a pokey flat back here in England, and

working in my friend's shop on minimum wage. I'm just so lonely again. It's like no one else can possibly understand what I'm feeling. And I'm ashamed to admit that I've started self-harming again, though I really don't want to any more. But how can I carry on when I have no self-worth; when I don't believe in myself?"

I took a deep breath and blew my nose, trying to control the sobbing.

"I believe in you, Jude," Annie said.

"I believe in you too," added the Great Raymondo.

"Me too," piped up Shane the Mane, his hairy hand patting my arm.

Annie picked up a pile of papers and began to hand one out to everyone. "Thank you, Jude, for sharing your story so openly. I know how painful it is to do that, especially when you don't yet know anyone. You're a very brave woman.

"Now, can anyone else relate to Jude's feeling of helplessness? Please raise your hand if you can."

Slowly but surely, everyone in the room put their hand in the air, including Annie.

"So I feel the time is right to look at Step One of our recovery programme." We all looked at our sheet.

"So, Step One then. *We admit that our life has become unmanageable and that alone, we are powerless.* Is everyone able to relate to this?"

We all nodded with a sense of mutual defeat, and I noticed I wasn't the only person to have shed a tear or few.

"Now, darlings, please let me explain that each of us here is part of a circle of hope that is far greater than any of our individual problems and differences. Together we are stronger.

"Please turn over your sheets and let's finish our meeting tonight by saying together the words of the Serenity Prayer."

Willingly, we all joined in, albeit with solemn voices:

"God, grant me

the serenity to accept the things I cannot change,
the courage to change the things I can,
and the wisdom to know the difference."

"May I thank you all from the bottom of my heart for showing up tonight. That's the most important thing you can do at the moment – show up. Because guess what? The healing process can't begin if you don't. I really hope to see you all again next week – same time, same place."

A few quiet but deeply meant thank yous were thrown Annie's way. Mousey Martha was the first to scurry out of the door, with the rest of us following closely behind.

I fell into my bed that night, exhausted by the resurfacing of all the emotions. But I also felt strangely cleansed, as though a big ball of knotted string had been released from my stomach. And although I never would have relished the thought of being the first group member to pour their heart out in front of a bunch of strangers, I was really glad I had. Maybe those metaphorical ten swords were beginning to lift from my back already.

Chapter Eight

I awoke with a jump. My skin was wet to the touch and my bedclothes were soaked through. I looked at the clock. It was three-thirty in the morning. The image of Matt and Deb, their bodies naked; writhing and grinding together, was still vivid in my mind. How could they? What had I done to deserve being treated like that by two of my most trusty soul mates? I had given him my mind, my body and my heart, not just partially but one hundred percent. I had allowed him to do whatever he wanted with me; nothing was off limits, and yet there he was, doing all those intimate things with someone else. And not just anyone else; my big sister. Maybe he found her more attractive. Maybe she smelt better, tasted better. Maybe her womanly curves were more seductive to him than my petite frame. Maybe she took the lead. Maybe she moaned louder.

I dug my fingernails in to my ankle, ripping the scab clean off, and watched the fresh blood creep to the surface.

* * *

Wednesday evening couldn't come soon enough, and I arrived to find the same faces sitting in the same seats as last week.

"Darlings, do make yourselves a hot drink – it's nippy in here tonight. And don't be too polite to dive into the tin of biscuits on the table. They're there to be eaten, and if *you* don't eat them, *I* will, and we can't have that now, can we?"

"Don't mind if I do," winked Shane the Mane, helping himself to a couple of chocolate digestives to accompany his strong black coffee.

I didn't usually drink caffeine in the afternoons, but I was feeling so knackered from a run of bad nights, that I made an exception. The rancid smell of the long-life milk aside, it felt comforting to be holding a warm drink between my chilly hands.

I wondered who would be the centre of attention tonight. Looking around, I could tell people felt anxious. At least I'd got the worst bit out of the way.

"So then, darlings, how are you all this week?" A few of the group nodded and muttered under their breaths that they were ok thanks. Others continued their assessment of the floor. "And, Jude, how have you felt after you bravely told us all about your story last time?"

Surprised to be in the spotlight yet again, I gripped my mug tightly. "Well, I felt pretty good straight after the session, as if I was already turning a corner. But then I started having some pretty disturbing dreams which really upset me, and I just feel exhausted now. I'm ashamed to say that I have caused pain to myself again since. I keep looking at Step One, and I totally agree that I feel powerless. So I guess I took a small step forward, followed by a couple of huge leaps back."

Annie nodded and smiled gently. "I can see how you would feel that way, darling, but believe me, you are not stepping backwards. You have, in actual fact, taken a huge leap forwards, and as a result, some uncomfortable feelings have risen to the surface to be dealt with. When these painful images or thoughts come up for us, we always have a choice. We can either bury them back down and ignore them, or we can look them in the face and work with them. Does that make sense?"

"Yes it does, thanks, Annie, although facing these demons isn't particularly easy is it?"

Annie laughed. "Whoever said recovery is easy was lying! It's not easy. It takes hard work, commitment, and plenty of surrendering. But believe me – it is possible. I've been in recovery for over thirty years, and I still have to return to my programme every day. Thank God I have a programme, or I don't know where I'd be. It's the only thing that keeps me sane!"

Annie didn't just look sane to me though. She looked happy.

Really happy.

The Great Raymondo sat forward in his chair and cleared his throat nervously. "Annie, you said last week that you were married to an alcoholic. Do you mind me asking how bad things got before you turned to Al-Anon?"

"Thanks for your question, Ray, and no, of course I don't mind sharing my story with you. Healing can only begin when we are completely honest with ourselves and each other.

"I married my lovely George when we were both twenty. He was a big man; taller than me, very handsome, and a wonderfully sweet-natured gentleman. Even through all of our turbulent times, I never once stopped loving him, nor he me.'

Raymondo smiled, as if he somehow understood.

"We often think of alcoholics as drop-outs, lying on a park bench with a brown paper bag, but this isn't the truth of the matter. Many people with very powerful jobs rely on drink to get them through. And George was no different. He had a responsible job and his staff and colleagues all loved him. But what they didn't know was that although he was working hard, the lovely George was also drinking all of our money away.

"We had two beautiful children, and I had to bring them up and also earn a decent enough wage to ensure that our bills were paid and that they didn't go without. But it wasn't all bad. George was a soft and loving husband and father. The sad thing was, he was completely powerless over drink.

"Reasoning with him never worked. Trying to make him feel bad about it never worked either. Interfering with him only made him drink more. My happiness became dependant on George not drinking, and his happiness became dependant on me being happy and not going on at him. We went round and round in circles like this for years, feeding the problem and making it worse. Nevertheless, we hung on in there.

"And then, out of the blue, at the age of forty, I had a massive heart attack that nearly killed me. I looked death in the face and

I realised that if I wanted to live, I had to make some changes to *my* lifestyle and *my* behaviour. After all, there was nothing I could do to change George's.

"I read something somewhere about Al-Anon, and so I phoned them for information, and was welcomed to join the nearest group. After all, my life *had* become unmanageable, and I *was* completely powerless – I had given it all away in my attempts to change the man I loved.

"Once I'd learnt the twelve-step recovery programme, I realised that the alcohol itself wasn't the problem. Taking alcohol out of the equation would not make everything ok. I had to take responsibility for my emotions and actions, and I had to allow George to take care of his.

"I asked my boss at work if I could have a two-hour lunch break every day so that I could go home, completely relax my body and mind, and regain perspective. Naturally I took less pay as a result, but you can't put a price on your health. If we don't have our health, then we don't have anything. So whether George was sober or drunk, I had to focus on me."

Annie stood up and began to hand out a sheet of paper to everyone.

"So, darlings, I first admitted I was powerless, and that my life was unmanageable. There was no question; I had to surrender. Now let's take a look at Step Two together. *We come to believe that a Power, greater than ourselves, can restore us to sanity.*

"So, how do we all feel about that statement? Do we see how we might need to pull on some extra resources to get through these turbulent times, like this group perhaps?"

Most people nodded, some said "yes".

"And do we feel up for supporting each other?" Everyone seemed to agree. "Ok, good. Right then, darlings, I'd like you all to focus your attention on the first two steps over the coming week. If things get tough, then all the more reason to turn to them, but please call me at any point if you need to. We mustn't be lonely.

"Now, if you want to make yourselves another hot drink before you leave, then please do. Take care, darlings, it's cold out there."

Wrapping my thick scarf around my neck and buttoning up my woolly coat, I found myself doing a quick scan of the room, and couldn't help noticing how faces were beginning to appear a little softer than they did earlier; even Mousey Martha's. Probably the relief of not having to pour their hearts out in front of everyone, I thought.

Chapter Nine

Feeling keen and fairly positive, I was the first to arrive at the third session.

"Jude! Lovely to see you," boomed Annie's large, confident voice enthusiastically. "Hasn't it been a glorious day? I've had some beautiful birds visit me in my garden today, including a rotund little robin I call George. I like to think my George still keeps an eye on me you see."

"How lovely, Annie. Robins are my favourite too. There's something quite magical about them." I decided to break the mould and sit in a different chair this week. Shane the Mane, however, sat in his usual seat, and in hindsight, I wished I'd done the same. I was now having to face him which I found rather creepy, but at least the potent combination of aftershave and testosterone weren't strangling my sinuses quite so much.

The last person to arrive was Mousey Martha; dressed in her usual muted tones. This week she sported a pair of thick brown trousers and a plain beige round-necked jumper. She held a hanky to her nose and it was pretty obvious that she'd been crying. She sat down as discreetly as she could, hoping to pass the tears off as a cold.

Perceptive as ever, Annie got straight to the point. "Welcome back, everyone. It's lovely to see you all, it really is. Now it looks as though today has been particularly difficult for Martha, so Martha, darling, if you feel up to telling us what's going on for you in your life at the moment, then perhaps we can offer you some support."

Martha nodded at the floor, giving her nose a quick blow and then folding her arms tightly across her body as if to cuddle herself. She took a deep breath in, and let out a hefty sigh, attempting to calm herself down. "It's my son. Michael. He's eighteen, and I'm ashamed to say that he's a…" Martha hesitated.

"...he's a drug user. He spends most of his time shut away in his room, which, to be honest, I can handle, 'cause at least I know where he is. But then there'll be a knock on the door, and you never know who's going to be there. We have all manner of unsavoury characters calling for Michael, and we've even had policemen turning up with their sniffer dogs to search our home. Very rarely do I answer the door to a friend of ours these days. I don't think anyone feels welcome to call in anymore.

"My husband and I are Christians. We haven't brought him up to be an addict and a thief, and I feel like a failure as a mother. Michael is our only child. We didn't think we could have children you see. And I guess we pinned all our hopes on him.

"He's a bright enough lad, but he's always hated school. Right from when he was little he never wanted to go. He was shy, you see; sensitive. And so he's come away with hardly a qualification to his name. I know that Michael's a lovely boy deep down, and I still love him very much, but I feel like we've lost him. We've lost our beautiful sweet boy to something that's so evil and so powerful."

Martha shook her head and blew her nose again. Annie passed her a tissue, having seen the soggy state of her hanky, and gestured for her to carry on.

"The reason I'm feeling so upset today, is that I noticed this morning that some cash had gone missing from my purse. It wasn't a fortune, but I'd got it out yesterday to pay the window cleaner, and the rest I was putting aside for the church's Christmas bazaar on Saturday. I just assumed my husband had borrowed it for his game of golf, but he hadn't. There was no other explanation. My own son had stolen from his mother, and it really hurts.

"No matter how much we tell him he's throwing his life away, he just carries on. He smiles and tells us not to worry, but really he couldn't care less.

"Every time he leaves the house, I turn myself inside out with worry, wondering if he's lying in a ditch somewhere, or robbing an old lady perhaps. It's as if he's been possessed by the Devil. This morning's episode was the last straw for my husband and he's threatened to throw Michael out if he doesn't clean up his act and start looking for a job. But that's my worst nightmare you see. Not knowing where he is; not knowing if and when we would see him again.

"Every day I rack my brains for the right words to use; words that will make him see what he's doing; words that will snap him out of it. He's so sucked in that I need to pull him out. I'm his mum and he's my responsibility.

"So, if anyone has any advice on what I can say or do, then please help me." Martha sobbed, clutching her elbows with her hands, and leaning forwards slightly as if her stomach was in pain. I felt so sorry for her and wished I could think of an answer.

"Thank you, Martha darling. I can feel your pain, I really can, and I'm sure we all appreciate your honesty."

Annie held up a battered paperback, covered in creases and stains. She took hold of her glasses that were hanging on a bright red chain around her neck, and raised them to sit at the end of her nose.

"I want to introduce you to a wonderful book called *The Language of Letting Go*. This morning, I flicked through the pages and asked that I stop on a page that will be most helpful for our meeting tonight. And if you don't mind, I'd like to read it to you…"

Responding to the nods around the room, and clearing her throat, Annie began reading the selected excerpt.

"How easy is it to blame our problems on others. 'Look at what he's doing' … 'Look how long I've waited' … 'Why doesn't she call?' … 'If only he'd change then I'd be happy' …

"Often our accusations are justified. We probably are feeling hurt and frustrated. In those moments, we may begin to believe that the solution to our pain and frustration is getting the other person to do

what we want, or having the outcome we desire. But these self-defeating illusions put the power and control of our life in other people's hands. We call this **codependency.**

"*The solution to our pain and frustration, however valid, is to acknowledge our own feelings. We feel the anger, the grief; then we let go of the feelings and find peace – within ourselves. We know our happiness isn't controlled by another person, even though we may have convinced ourselves it is. We call this* **acceptance.**

"*Then we decide that although we'd like our situation to be different, maybe our life is happening this way for a reason. Maybe there is a higher purpose and plan in play, one that's better than we could have orchestrated. We call this* **faith.**

"*Then we decide what we need to do, what is within our power to do to take care of ourselves. That's called* **recovery.**

"*It's easy to point our finger at another, but it's more rewarding to gently point it at ourselves.*"

Annie closed her book gently and removed the glasses from her nose.

There was no doubt about it; these words had affected everyone in the room in one way or another. Martha sobbed quietly into her now soggy tissue. Shane the Mane looked to the floor and frowned. The Great Raymondo nodded gently in agreement. And I felt myself smile; realising the truth in this wisdom.

It made perfect sense to me. I had spent so much of my life trying to please others and hoping that they would behave lovingly towards me in return, that I had given away nearly all of my power. No wonder I felt so miserable and empty.

Wherever would I be without Annie? Without a doubt, she was my teacher.

"So, darlings, let's talk about the addict now. It doesn't matter what the addiction is. Whether it's drugs, alcohol, unhealthy relationships, pornography; it is almost irrelevant. People abuse themselves because they are sad inside, and they use their addiction as a coping mechanism; something that might just fill this empty void that they are feeling.

"Firstly, we must understand that the addict is ill, and that they are far too self-absorbed to realise, worry or care about what someone else is going through.

"Secondly, these people need and deserve love and affection – even if they have turned to crime; it doesn't mean we cannot or must not love them. It is perfectly ok to love an addict, but we *must* focus on loving ourselves. When we love ourselves, we come to understand our limitations; what is acceptable to us and what is unacceptable.

"When we are totally engrossed and caught up in someone else's addiction, it means we are in denial, and also that we are not living our own lives. It is not the alcohol or drugs that are the real problem; it is the unacceptable behaviour of the addict. If the behaviour is not acceptable to you, then the addiction is a problem.

"So, together, my darlings, we *must* work on the issue of boundaries. What is acceptable and what is not? We simply cannot allow ourselves to be pushed beyond our own limitations, or we will quite simply break.

"Now then, let's think back to our Serenity Prayer. We ask for the serenity to accept the things we cannot change and, Martha, darling, you absolutely do not have the power to single-handedly change your son's behaviour or situation. Can we all see that?"

Everyone agreed.

"So this brings us nicely on to Step Three of our programme: *We make a decision to turn our will and our lives over to the care of God as we understand Him.*"

Shane the Mane crossed his legs, folded his arms and looked to the ceiling.

"Now, Martha, you kindly shared with us that you follow the Christian faith, and so this step is really about surrendering to your God and letting him handle your situation for you.

"But, darlings, please don't think I'm trying to convert you into following a religion. I am absolutely not. In fact, I am not religious myself. But I *do* believe in a higher power; a power that is greater than me. And so whether your God is a religious figure, whether it's Mother Nature, whether it's the Man in the Moon, whether it's the brightest star in the sky, whether it's your Higher Self, or anything else for that matter, then that's fine. Just so long as you can put your faith in something wonderful that you believe in.

"Now, I understand that some of you may need some time to get used to this concept, but believe me; it's so helpful if you can. It allows us to start letting go.

"So, over the coming week, please continue to focus on the first two steps and really think about how you can best make Step Three meaningful to you. If you want to call me at any point meantime to discuss this or anything else, then please do."

* * *

I sat staring out of the bus window and into the dark night sky, contemplating what God could mean for me. I hadn't been one for religion ever since I attended my first-ever family christening service, where the vicar went on about us all being born as sinners until we rise with Christ through a christening, and how the godparents (in this case a shifty-looking male friend of the father's, and a bimbo in her early twenties, dressed head to toe in designer bling) would show him the way.

I remember sitting there, looking at my cousin's child; this bouncing bundle of smiling innocence, and wondering how he could possibly be viewed as anything other than pure love. If this concept was true, then surely babies would be born with demonic eyes or disturbing grimaces and then, once christened, transform into angelic beings of grace and beauty. Only as I saw it, most babies were born adorable and soon turned into selfish little shits as they matured, christened or not. I wondered whether Mousey Martha's Michael had been christened. More than likely, I reckoned.

But although I wasn't a fan of structured rules and regulations, I did often feel that a power far greater than me was at work. I only wished that he, she or it would work a bit harder in my favour sometimes, that's all. I thought back to the image of the gurgling baby (who unfortunately was now a well-known expert in the art of graffiti).

Pure Love, I thought. *That can be my God.*

Chapter Ten

It was ten in the morning and the frost remained heavy on the ground. I always started work late on a Thursday as it tended to be our quietest day in the shop. As I walked through the door, I noticed an unopened deck of cards sitting on the counter.

"Oh, brilliant, they've arrived! How exciting! Did Rose drop these in this morning, Saff?" I was so busy ripping open the seal that I didn't even notice that Saffie was crying in the kitchen. She emerged, massaging her temples, her eyes all red and blotchy.

"Yes, she called in first thing. I gave her the money from the till."

"Saff! Whatever's wrong?" Saffie was usually so upbeat and jovial, that it was hard to see her when she wasn't. She hadn't looked this upset since Martin had left her so I guessed it had to be bad.

"Oh, it's money, Jude. The landlord's just announced he's putting the rental up, and I'm struggling to make ends meet as it is. I just don't think I have the time or the energy to get the business to the level it needs to be at. Sol might be growing up fast, but he still needs me and he deserves my attention."

She shrugged her shoulders and rolled her head around in a circle, as if to release some tension.

"Anyway, I'm sorry, honey. I didn't want to put this on you; you've got enough on your plate, and I don't want you losing sleep, worrying about your job as well. It'll be ok. I'll sort it somehow."

I gave her a hug, giving her back a soothing rub.

"Look, why don't you go home, catch up on some sleep, and make a nice hearty dinner for you and Sol. Put a movie on and snuggle up together on the sofa tonight. I can take care of things here, and I guarantee you'll feel a whole lot better for a good rest. Then when you feel a bit stronger, you can think about the shop.

What do you reckon?"

Saffie sighed, nodded in agreement, grabbed her keys and gave me a kiss. "Thanks, Judith. Whatever would I do without you?"

"Ditto, my friend. Now go get some sleep."

A rush of bitterly cold air blew in as the door closed behind her. I lifted the lid of the jewel-coloured box, its edges embossed with gold swirls, and removed the cards. They smelt fresh and crisp, and my hand tingled as I held them. They had been accompanied by a note from Rose, explaining that these weren't the same as hers, but quite literally fell off the shop shelf in front of her, and had a really wonderful energy that felt perfect for me.

With Saffie and the shop clearly in my mind, I shuffled the deck and laid them all face down on the counter. One card stood out from the rest, as if it was reaching its hand up, saying 'pick me, pick me!' I pushed it out with my finger and turned it over.

Looking up at me was an image of two figures standing closely together, with the words 'PARTNERSHIP – two heads are better than one' written below.

Feeling thrilled and thankful for the answer, I messaged Saffie straight away: *'The cards say you need a partner to invest in the business.'*

And a few minutes later, I got a reply: *'Thanks, Jude, that's sweet of you, though I really can't think of anyone who has the money to help me.'*

Feeling sure that this card had appeared for a reason, I did something I'd never done before. I began to pray.

"Pure Love, please help me to support Saffie in her hour of need. Please help her to find a way to keep her lovely business going so that she can provide a comfortable life for herself and her son. Thank you."

* * *

The mood in the room was slightly lighter this week and we welcomed one another with gentle hellos rather than avoiding each others' gazes. Maybe we were starting to relax into the safety of the group. After all, it was becoming a bit of a dependable crutch for most, if not all of us.

Annie sat in her usual place, her surrounding circumference littered with an array of papers, pens, rulers and magazines. She was dressed in autumnal shades of burnt orange, dark red and sage green, making her presence well known as usual.

"Good evening, darlings. It's so lovely to see you here as always, and I hope you're all managing to work with the first three steps to some degree.

"Now, I'm sure Ray won't mind me telling you that he felt the need to call me during the week as he was feeling particularly anxious and couldn't wait until tonight to get some support.

"So, Ray, darling, do you feel happy to share what's happening in your life with the group, and perhaps we can help?"

The Great Raymondo laughed nervously. "Oh, ok then. Well, to give you a bit of background, I've been married to my wife, Maria, for twenty-seven years. We are both Jewish and are fairly traditional in that Maria has always stayed at home, and I've always been the breadwinner. And like many Jewish wives, Maria is the holder of the purse strings. We were never blessed with children so it's just the two of us, although Maria has always been my baby really.

"She is a wonderful woman and I adore her, but the trouble is that she is rather partial to the finer things in life. The kind of things we can't really afford. I've always worked hard, as I like to please my wife and give her what she wants, but I have reached the conclusion that no matter how much I earn, or how much we have, she will keep wanting more.

"We live in a massive house, she buys new cars every year, she dresses from head to toe in designer gear, and is forever getting her nails done or her eyelashes done, or her hair done. She books us on all these exotic holidays, she hires architects and builders and interior designers and gardeners without my agreement, and she spends many a lunchtime socialising with her friends in our local health club, eating lavishly and drinking lots of expensive wine.

"Now don't get me wrong. I'm very happy for her to have all of these things, but her spending is getting more and more out of hand, and our debts are starting to feel insurmountable. I just can't keep up with it, but I'm frightened to tell her in case she leaves me for someone else who *is* able to provide the kind of lifestyle she wants.

"So I came along to this group because I feel like my life is out of control. I've buried my head in the sand for a long, long time, and as a result, I'm now suffocating.

"The reason why I felt the need to phone Annie this week, is because I have just discovered that my job's on the line, and I'm waiting to hear whether it'll be me or the other director in the company that gets made redundant.

"God knows what I'll do if it's me. I'm fifty-five years old. I daren't tell Maria; she'll be mortified. So I guess, like many of you, I feel very lonely at the moment. Lonely and seriously frightened. The denial hasn't worked, so I have to find a new way."

The Devil card from Rose's reading popped into my mind as Raymondo was talking. It was if he was merrily dancing along to his wife's tune, becoming more and more trapped by fear. I could really resonate with him. After all, my relationships tended to be based around me pleasing others too.

The Great Raymondo seemed like a nice chap. Very smiley and kind. He certainly didn't deserve to be treated like that. But then again, neither did I.

"Well, thank you, Ray, for sharing your story with us all. As you can probably tell by now, it doesn't matter whether the issue is based around alcohol, drugs, compulsive spending, co-dependency or anything else; the point is that people turn to these behaviours when they are trying to fill a void. So, Ray, what void do you think your wife Maria is trying to fill by spending, spending, spending?" Annie asked.

"I think it's probably sadness because we could never have children. We've never really spoken about it at length, and to be honest, I've always been frightened to, for fear of upsetting her."

"There's always a reason, darling, and it's always based around fear. So perhaps then your wife is afraid of lack.

"Now then, an important point to make is that, no matter how hard we try; no matter what we say or do, or how loud we shout, we simply cannot change the addict's behaviour. What we can do, however, is change ourselves."

Annie stood up and handed out a couple of sheets of paper, a magazine, a pen and a ruler to everyone.

"How did we all get on with the God concept of Step Three last week? Were you all able to find someone or something that could be your God?"

Most of us nodded, but Shane the Mane admitted to having struggled with this one. Annie suggested they have a chat at the end as this wasn't at all uncommon.

"So, darlings, let's now look at Step Four together: *We make a searching and fearless moral inventory of ourselves.*

"Now then, it's only when we've made the commitment to turn our will and our lives over to the care of God as we understand Him, that we can really begin to carry out Step Four effectively." She looked around the room, as if to gauge people's reactions. "But I think it's an exercise worth touching on this evening if you're ready. And you will know as soon as you start whether you are ready or not.

"Before we begin, I'd like to share my experience of Step Four with you if I may.

"When I joined Al-Anon, I was convinced that George's

drinking was the problem. It was something that *he* was doing, not me. It was *his* fault and I was pretty much perfect. But then, through Al-Anon, I began to learn that the role *I* played was also part of the problem. And although this was very hard to admit to, it also gave me something to work with. I could begin to change myself.

"I soon realised that some of my best intentions were actually my flaws; the things that got me into most trouble. And I began to learn about the part that I played in George's alcoholism, which actually helped to feed his disease. I saw for the first time that my actions in trying to look after him were actually preventing him from taking care of himself.

"Now believe me, darlings, this step is not an easy one. It can be very painful and raw, bringing all sorts of gunge to the surface. But it is also enlightening and freeing, not to mention a very necessary step towards recovery.

"So, whether you yourself have the drink problem, or you are the loved one of the drinker, we are all in fact addicts of unhealthy behaviour. Otherwise we wouldn't be sitting here. And that's pretty tough to hear and to come to terms with.

"May I also add that I continue to this day to carry out a searching and fearless moral inventory of myself on a daily basis. Our work is never done while we are still here on this earth.

"So, only if you feel ready, and using your magazine to rest on, I'd like you to draw a line down the centre of your sheet and on one side write the title 'my positive attributes' and on the other side write 'my flaws'. And then begin to write down all the things about yourself which you consider to be your strengths. Perhaps you're caring for example, or thoughtful.

"And then on the opposite side of the sheet, really think about how these positive attributes could become negative if taken to the extreme. For example, you are caring, but you care too much and this may prevent someone caring for themselves.

"I must add that this is not about judging or beating ourselves up, and neither is it about feeding the ego. None of us are perfect. We never will be. But we *can* be better; especially if we accept and let go of our destructive behaviours."

Whilst listening to Annie's words, a light bulb moment suddenly occurred. Hand on heart, up until then, I had truly believed that all the bad things which had happened in my life had been unfairly thrown at me and I couldn't understand why. I had never once considered that my actions may also have played a significant part.

Perhaps life wasn't so cruel after all. And maybe, if I could summon up the strength to make some changes to the way *I* behaved, then I could stop feeling like the victim. I could stop dancing to the Devil's tune and begin to live again.

Chapter Eleven

I lit a candle and shuffled my deck. "Pure Love, please guide me with a loving message for my day ahead."

I had never really asked for higher guidance in the past, but since my reading with Rose and my sessions with Annie, it suddenly felt like a natural thing to do. I loved my new cards; they really spoke to me, and they helped add a new positive dimension to my life.

As I shuffled away, a card flew out and landed on the floor in front of me. Staring up at me was a beautiful woman with long red hair and bright sparkly green eyes. She was surrounded by four-leafed clovers and was holding something out to me. Beneath her were the words 'LADY LUCK IS WITH YOU – open your arms to receive'.

Not a bad start to the day, I thought. I could do with some good fortune. "Ok then, Lady Luck, my arms are open to you," I said aloud, and deliberated on whether to buy my lottery ticket before or after work.

Wednesday had soon come around again, and I was feeling much lighter having worked with the four steps we'd learnt so far. I certainly felt less lonely, and also positive in the knowledge that I could transform my own behaviour for the better. I had made a conscious decision not to read up on the eight remaining steps as I think I would have felt overwhelmed. But at the same time, I was keen to discover what was coming next.

Annie gave us all a warm welcome as usual. "Well, darlings, we have much to cover this evening, but before I run away with myself, I'd like to know whether you are all ok with the use of the term God? What does God mean for you?" She turned her attention to Shane the Mane who didn't seem so closed off this week.

"I think I've got my head around it now thanks, Annie. Our

chat last week definitely helped, and I feel very comfortable to picture my late mum when I say the word God. I hope she's looking down on me and I feel able to ask her for help. I was only twenty when she passed away and I still miss her every day. She was a wonderful woman – loving and brave...all the things I'm not really."

Annie sat forward with interest, her large bust, encased in a scarlet red jumper, protruding ahead all the more. "Well that's fabulous, darling. We just need to find something that feels right for us. Is everyone else ok with that?'

We all nodded happily.

"Right then. I think it's time to discuss Step Five: *We admit to God, to ourselves, and to another human being, the exact nature of our wrongs.*"

She peered up from her glasses, glancing around the room, checking our reactions. "So, folks, another big ask. How do we feel about this one? Would anyone like to share?"

Shane the Mane raised his hand. He seemed to have left the bravado at home this week and looked somewhat downtrodden.

"Annie, the thought of this step scares the hell out of me. I really don't want to go there, but I know I'll have to if I want to change. And believe me, I do. I've had enough of living like this."

"Well, darling, that's perfectly natural. Resistance will most definitely come into play with this step for all of us. Now, Shane, do you feel up to sharing your difficulties with the group?"

Shane nodded, realising it was now or never.

"Yeah, ok. Well, my issue is that I rely on women, pornography and sex to pick me up."

Mousey Martha looked uncomfortable, turning her knees in the opposite direction.

"Whenever I feel low, I head out to one of the local bars, and pick up a woman. There's always plenty of them about; unhappy housewives, looking for a bit of attention, all dressed up, you know.

"Don't get me wrong, I don't treat them badly or anything. I give 'em a good time and we have a laugh, but I never give them my number. I never want to get close to them emotionally. It's just a physical desire that makes me feel manly and worthwhile at the time. Women are beautiful creatures, but they are dangerous too, so an even safer option is to watch them on screen, and get off on that, but when all the fun is over, I just feel cheap and even worse than before. And so the cycle continues – I go out looking for a woman who might just make me feel a bit better about myself.

"The trouble is, I'm forty-seven now. I don't want to live this way any more. But this addiction is hard to break, and I need help.

"Now, what you say about Step Five freaks me right out. It's bad enough admitting to you guys that I'm addicted to sex and porn, and use women for their bodies, but to admit this to my God, my mum, who would probably be mortified at the way I'm living, is making me feel physically sick. I guess that means I make myself feel sick really."

Annie interjected, "Don't forget, darling, we're talking about our behaviour, and we all have the power to change our behaviour. What you've just done is very brave. It takes great courage to stand there and admit you're not perfect. And that does make you a man, Shane, it really does. And I'm sure we all respect you for that. We are not here to judge you or anyone else. We are here to help and support."

Annie turned to the group. "So, leading on from Shane's sharing, let us also look at Step Six: *We are entirely ready to have God remove all these defects of character.*

"Are we ready to do this?

"Because when, and only when, we are ready to surrender in this way, we can combine Steps Six and Seven: *By humbly asking Him to remove our shortcomings.*

"Now this is something I'd like you to go home and work on

this week. As always, please don't hesitate to call if you're struggling with anything."

She handed us all a sheet with Steps Five to Seven boldly printed on it, and sent us on our way.

* * *

I decided to ring the bus bell a stop early so I could buy a lottery ticket from the late-night newsagent's. Feeling lucky, I pushed the boat out and bought myself two.

The extra walk home was bitterly cold, and I hoped my 'investment' had been worth it. I pushed open the door to find a handwritten letter on the mat, peeking out from the less interesting-looking items of mail.

My stomach churned with anxiety and disbelief as I recognised the writing. The card was from Deb. Just when I started to feel a little more in control of things, my sister decides to show up and shove those painful images back in my face. So much for Lady Luck.

I peeled open the envelope, dreading whatever lay inside. I was greeted by the words on the front of the card: 'I'm Sorry', with a picture of a cute puppy glancing upwards at me. As I opened it, a piece of paper flew out and onto the sofa. I'd get to that in a moment, I thought, and focused my attention on Deb's message:

Dear Jude,

I hope you're ok. I really am so very sorry for what happened. I don't know what I was thinking and I feel awful about it.

Anyway, I'm not writing for your forgiveness, but I wanted you to know that I've decided to move closer to Mum and have put Dad's house on the market. Obviously, you are entitled to half, so I'll let you know when the sale has completed and we can sort this out.

Meanwhile, Dad's premium bonds finally paid out and he won

£14,000 in this month's draw! I'd like you to have the money, Jude – the cheque's enclosed.

I'll be in touch.

Deb xxx

Chapter Twelve

We arrived to find the village hall lights dimmed low, with flickering candles dotted around the room, and gentle music playing softly in the background.

At the foot of our seats lay a piece of paper and a pen, which led us to conclude that we weren't just here for a rest; there was more work to be done.

"Right, darlings, I'd like you all to remove your shoes and pop them under your chairs please. We're going to start the evening off with a meditation.

"Now get yourselves comfy, rest your hands in your laps, and close your eyes. Begin to breathe deeply and slowly, allowing your body and mind to relax. Feel your feet flat on the solid ground beneath you.

"If you feel comfortable to, please ask your God as you understand Him to be present with you, and feel safe in the knowledge that you are not alone.

"Now I'd like you to bring into your mind, anyone who you think you may have harmed during your journey to this present day, and allow those images to come forward. Don't fight against them, or allow your mental dialogue to take over, just let them be with you and your God. Keep your heart open and breathe these feelings in. Don't be afraid. These feelings are part of you.

"Now, when you feel ready, begin to bring your attention back to the room, opening your eyes. And if you feel ok to do so, please make a list of anyone who showed up as being someone you may have harmed."

I opened my eyes from what had been an enlightening experience. During the meditation, I had come to realise that I may have harmed my family for not involving them in my wedding, and for moving away to India without much contact. I could see why Deb might have felt pushed out, and then jealous when Dad became ill and wanted me with him. Maybe she even blamed me on some level for his illness.

And maybe I had harmed Matt greatly by giving him all of my undivided attention, and then taking it away from him in an instant, leaving him to fend for himself.

I was so engrossed in my realisation and in my list-writing that I was oblivious to what anyone else was doing. Annie, however, was not.

"Martha, darling, are you ok? Can I help you with anything?"

I glanced up to find Mousey Martha looking furious, her face red and her arms firmly crossed. In the short time I had known her, she'd never looked so colourful or interesting. "I'm sorry, Annie, but I really do not see why I should sit here feeling bad, when it's my son who's at fault."

Annie smiled gently. "This exercise is not about anyone judging you, Martha, we are simply reviewing our own actions, to realise our own part in our difficult situations. If you honestly feel you have harmed no one along your journey of struggle, then that's fine, although it *is* rather unusual. Do you think you may have possibly harmed yourself though, darling?"

Martha shook her head and rose to her feet. "My son is the one who's hurt me, not the other way around. This isn't my fault. I'm a good mother and I came here looking for support, not to make myself feel worse!" She grabbed her coat and stormed towards the door, returning quickly for her boots which she'd forgotten, much to her annoyance.

"And support is exactly what you will receive here, Martha. Support from people who understand your pain and who care about your recovery."

Wrestling with her boots, she pointed an angry finger at Shane the Mane. "How can someone like *him* possibly understand how I feel?"

She turned on her heels and stormed out of the room, leaving an air of awkwardness behind her. Ok, granted, Shane *did* come across as a bit of a perv, but he didn't deserve that.

"Darlings, please don't worry. This is all part of recovery. We are all bound to have our wobbles over the coming weeks and months, and Martha, bless her heart, is just having one of hers now.

"But like everything that happens, this too shall pass. We must understand and continue to remember that fact. Martha's comments were made, and they are now a thing of the past. Let's send her the love that she so needs at the moment to help her through her struggles.

"Shane, darling, please try not to take that personally. Martha is *really* annoyed with herself, not you. You were just unfortunately picked to be her target. But just because she's thrown her frustration at you, it doesn't mean you have to catch it. We always have a choice you see."

Shane's jaw slowly began to close, and I think he felt comforted by the rest of our supportive smiles of empathy.

"So let's take a look together now at Step Eight: *We make a list of all persons we have harmed, and become willing to make amends to them all.*

"Now, darlings, this step really *does* take courage. The aim is not to punish ourselves, but rather to set ourselves free from any feelings of guilt and fear that we may be carrying. When we release these fears, then healing can begin, and this is a truly wonderful thing.

"Actually, it is highly likely that we have harmed ourselves more than anyone else along the way, so let's all put our own names at the top of our list.

"Now, you may feel you need lots more time to finish writing your list, so please don't feel pressured to get it all done tonight. This list is for you, not me or anyone else, but believe me, it's an important thing to do.

"And it's also important to keep referring to your list and adding to it whenever you need to. We must keep on returning to our twelve-step programme as it is the thing that will restore us to sanity.

"So now I'm going to ask something even bigger of you. Step Nine: *We make direct amends to such people wherever possible, except when doing so would injure them or others.*

"How do we feel about this one, darlings?"

Crikey! This one certainly got me thinking, and I felt some need for guidance. "My question, Annie, is that if I have realised my part in hurting another, but they have hurt me a hundred times more, should I still try to make amends?"

Annie nodded. "Aha, yes! An excellent question, Jude. 'I may have hurt them, but they hurt me more, so surely they should apologise first, right?' This attitude actually leads us into co-dependency. We become dependant on the other person putting their behaviour right so that we don't have to. Believe me, darling, this way of looking at things is very disempowering, and this is exactly what our lovely Martha is experiencing at the moment.

"Now let's not forget that we feel angry with someone for a reason, and we must acknowledge, honour, and experience these feelings fully. But we must also find a way to let them go, and this can be very difficult indeed. Perhaps if we let them go, we will get hurt again.

"But there are two things we can do here. Firstly we can set new boundaries to protect ourselves in the future, and secondly we can make amends for our own part by looking to, and changing, our own behaviour."

Shane raised his hand. "So, does making amends mean saying sorry? I mean, I'm ashamed to say that this won't be physically possible for me, as I wouldn't know where to find them all."

Annie chuckled kindly. "Sometimes yes, darling, but not necessarily. And this is where we must trust our own intuition, or higher power, to guide us into doing what feels right. Above all, we need to let go of any defensive feelings of anger or guilt, and replace them instead with the healing energy that is love. If you're not able to say sorry to the person you've harmed, then perhaps you could write a letter of apology for example, and then burn it when you've finished. This way, you have admitted your fault, apologised to it, and then let it go. How does that sound?"

"That makes sense, Annie. I'll definitely give that some thought."

As I travelled home that evening, Meeta popped into my mind. She had been such a wonderful friend to me, and given me so much love, and yet I had left *her* in an instant too, without even a call or an explanation, and I had never really considered how hurtful that must've been.

And dear old Gulab too. She had invested so much time in me; teaching me her cooking skills and looking forward to my visits, and yet I had disappeared from her life in a flash also.

I knew they would have understood my situation and supported me one hundred percent in my efforts to be with my dad, but that wasn't the point. I had never taken the time to explain, or even offer a forwarding address, and that was unacceptable. I added them to my list.

So that's where I would begin. I would write to Meeta and Gulab with an apology, and to find out how they both were. They may have wished to support me in my hour of need, and I was so busy wallowing in my sad state of aloneness, that I hadn't even given them the opportunity.

I felt sure that this was the right thing to do, and so with an open heart that felt full of love, I began to write to these beautiful souls, apologising for my elusiveness, and telling them how much they meant to me. I also vowed that as soon as I had some money and got all of my finances in order, I would either return to Punjab for a visit, or invite them to stay with me, whichever they preferred.

Knowing I might be able to do some good and share some love with Dad's hard-earned money felt amazing, and as I sealed the envelopes, a feeling of freedom washed over me, as if the chains were beginning to slacken.

Chapter Thirteen

In the weeks that passed, it was difficult to watch Saffie struggle, and although I had hope in my heart that I might soon be able to help her, I wasn't sure exactly when or how to, and so I chose to just listen for now, and to offer her hugs. I somehow knew that when the time was right, I would be shown what to do, but the last thing I wanted meantime was to give her false hope.

The recovery programme was certainly helping me to think more about the consequences of my actions, and this, in turn, was allowing healthier boundaries to emerge.

Our next session seemed like a bit of a milestone, which reflected the way I was feeling. It was good to see Mousey Martha back, but although her return had taken great courage, she *did* look incredibly embarrassed and even mousier than usual. It transpired that she had phoned Annie the following morning in a right old state. They'd consequently met up and talked things through. Thank Pure Love she had Annie, I thought. I wondered where on earth we would be without this awesome woman. She truly was a force like no other.

"Well, darlings. We are all making wonderful progress and I'd like to take this opportunity to commend you for your commitment – to the programme, to each other, and most impor-tantly, to yourselves. It's a privilege to be part of your journey, it really is.

"Now then, when we have taken on board and worked through the first nine steps, and continue to be mindful of steps one to nine, we can begin to maintain these ways of helping ourselves with the last three steps.

"Let me be very clear about it; we can't all be ready for this at the same time, but let's begin to discuss them anyway, so we all know what we're aiming for."

She handed us all a sheet of paper to add to our collection.

"Step Ten: *We continue with our personal inventories and when we are wrong, we promptly admit to it.*

"Now then, let's think back over the last week. Is anyone brave enough to confess to any wrongdoings that are leaving you feeling bad?"

Shane reluctantly raised his hand. "Well I must admit to you all, I felt completely shit about myself after that inventory thing last week, especially after what Martha said to me."

Her chest and ears turning flame red, Martha sat forward in her chair. "I'm sorry for what I said to you, Shane. It was unforgiveable. I wrongly judged you and I sincerely apologise. It was most un-Christian of me."

Annie looked approvingly at Martha and turned her attention back to Shane who was slightly taken aback.

"Well, ok. Thanks, Martha. Apology accepted, I guess.

"Anyway, on my way home that night, and I feel embarrassed to admit this, but I went straight to the pub and had meaningless sex with a woman I'd never met. Don't get me wrong, she was a willing participant and we both enjoyed the moment. But the reality is that I banged some lady's brains out in a cold, dark corridor. Not exactly very loving of me was it?

"Probably made her feel wanted and womanly for a few minutes, but afterwards, it just felt wrong. I felt guilty and ashamed that I'd allowed this urge to take over again, and really bad that I'd involved someone else in that too; some poor vulnerable woman who was unhappy like me. I felt like I'd gone back to square one again, and I feel really shit for letting all of you down too."

Annie nodded, not looking in the slightest bit shocked or embarrassed, but rather as if she'd heard it all before.

"I see, darling. Well, thank you for your honesty, and I can tell you right now that you have certainly not returned to square one, as you are now fully aware of the consequences and you have openly admitted your wrongdoings. So the thing to do now is to return to the steps, and make your amends in whatever way you can."

Shane looked grateful for Annie's advice.

Martha interjected again. "I feel partly responsible for Shane's downfall last week," to which Annie replied, "Shane is responsible for Shane's actions, Martha, and you are responsible for yours. So please do whatever you feel is right to not feel guilty, but rather to make amends."

It was heart-warming to watch Shane's and Martha's eyes meet in a reassuring look of positivity and humility. They had both been stripped to the core in accepting their shortcomings, and I had a funny feeling that this would be the start of a solid and beautiful friendship.

Chapter Fourteen

We all sat round in our familiar circle, having made ourselves a hot drink and helped ourselves to a piece of Mousey Martha's lemon drizzle cake which she'd made the day before as a peace offering.

It was pleasant enough but lacked the kind of zing that makes your lips purse. I wondered whether Martha's cakes would become more fruity as she continued to let go of her issues, but then quickly felt mean for judging her kindness and generosity.

Our drinks had been drunk and our cake eaten, but there was still a seat that remained empty. It was Annie's.

Feeling more at ease with each other by now, we chatted amongst ourselves, swapping stories on how we'd each come to meet Annie in unexpected circumstances, agreeing that she was probably an Earth Angel. Shane had met her in a long queue at the petrol station, Martha was approached by her at the local bakery, and Ray had met her by the cash machine where she found him in a panic. It was quite amazing really.

Almost half an hour had passed when an unfamiliar face entered the room; a chap in his mid- to late-thirties, I guessed, with a friendly smile and a nice vibe about him. He removed his leather jacket and hung it over the back of Annie's chair.

"Hi, everyone, my name's Guy and no, I'm not some random bloke gatecrashing your meeting! I'm blessed and honoured to say that Annie is a wonderful and very dear friend of mine. Sadly, our lovely Annie is in hospital at the moment having had a heart attack yesterday morning, but despite how sick and weak she's feeling, it was so important to her that this meeting went ahead, and she's asked that I come along and share my story with you, so I hope you don't mind. Please feel free to chip in and ask questions at any point."

Several surprised gasps filled the room; shocked at the

thought of Annie, our strong leader, being far too ill to attend.

Guy had sparkly brown eyes and he looked confident and together. I was intrigued to hear what he'd been through. With several keen pairs of ears seeming ready to listen, he sat down in a relaxed position and started to speak.

"I'm very pleased to say that today, life is good. But it hasn't always been this way. For many years, an addiction to alcohol stripped away everything I had, and harmed the lives of many people around me."

"Goodness gracious," Martha interjected. "Forgive me for saying, but you really don't look like someone who's had a drink problem."

Guy smiled tenderly. "I think many people's perception of an alcoholic is some kind of drop out. But in actual fact, it's very often people who are incredibly successful and intelligent who have problems with addictions."

Martha raised her chin and sat back in her seat, nodding for Guy to continue.

"From a young age, I remember feeling very different from other people; very insecure and inferior. I sometimes wonder if I was even born an alcoholic; who knows.

"My childhood was challenging. I watched my dad batter my mum who I loved dearly, and also abuse my sisters. And strangely, despite all this, I actually craved his love and attention, feeling somehow left out.

"There was a big hole in my soul for many years, and around the time I started working and earning money, alcohol became a close friend to me. It filled a big void and it soothed my sadness. For the first time ever, I went from feeling like a shrivelled up little mouse, to a courageous lion. I loved drink, and drink loved me. It was an intense love affair and nothing else could come close.

"I moved to Australia a few years later and being a bit of a clown when under the influence, I soon became known locally as the Beach Boozer. It wasn't long before the blackouts started and I began to lose days at a time; a result which quickly turned into my main aim.

"My ego became huge and I quickly transformed into a selfish, self-seeking, self-pitying nightmare. 'Poor-me' was my motto. I lost all of my dignity, and for many years, I treated everyone around me like pieces of crap.

"All of my relationships with women followed the same repetitive cycle; good for a few months, and then as soon as they got too close and started to interfere with my drinking, then Heaven help them; they all got kicked into touch. Either that, or I'd just go missing for days on end. Women and relationships simply couldn't match the way that booze made me feel.

"I remember one girlfriend of mine announced she was going away on holiday with her folks, and asked me to pop in and feed their cat whilst they were gone. I agreed, seeing this as an ideal opportunity to go on a complete bender. I cleared out their drinks cabinet for them, didn't feed the cat – not even once, and her parents returned to find me blacked out in their bed. Needless to say, I had to face the wrath of her dad! But *I* didn't have a problem; it was everyone else."

I couldn't resist. I had to ask, "So, what happened to the cat? Did it die?"

Guy chuckled. "Fortunately not. It must've had plenty of lives left I reckon. The cat was fine.One less thing on my conscience at least!" I smiled, feeling glad to have my question resolved, and allowed Guy to continue.

"Anyway, things got dark, and one night in Sydney, I phoned my mum to tell her that within the hour, her son would be dead, and having delivered this message, I promptly hung up. The poor woman was on the other side of the world and completely helpless. I took a cocktail of alcohol and tablets and was later found by my girlfriend at the time who got me rushed into A&E. That's how completely selfish I was. But I still couldn't see that I had a problem; it was still everyone else's fault.

"So did it get better, I hear you ask? No, no, it got much worse.

"I decided to take myself on an adventure to Asia for two months. It was going to be great. My first stop was Bangkok. In fact, this turned out to be the only stop. I spent the whole two months in my hotel bedroom, practically chained to the bed, accompanied by my best friend, booze, ordering it all from room service until they refused to serve me any more. By this time, I was in such a state, a quivering wreck in my bed, and too much of a mess to go out, that I resorted to eating cigarette butts off the floor. But I still didn't think it was a problem.

"After my so called 'adventure', I flew back home to live with my mum in the UK who hadn't heard from me in months and had thought me probably dead. I didn't care about any of this trivial shit; my only focus was to get smashed and black out.

"I started freelancing in London, working sober during the week, and looking forward to the weekends when I could booze continuously. It wasn't long before I'd get up for work on a Monday morning, and before I stepped on the tube, a little voice would say to me, 'Don't go in today, Guy. Take the day off. Have a drink, you deserve it.' So I'd pop to the off-license, skip work, and drink in bed all day instead. And because my work was so good when I *was* at work, I got away with this behaviour for quite some time.

"It was at a mate's stag weekend, when I threw myself into a three-foot swimming pool, behaving like the clown as usual, that one of my friends called me an alcoholic. I went ballistic at him. What a load of rubbish. What the hell did he know? Arsehole."

"It must have taken courage for your friend to say that to you, Guy. Did his words penetrate in some way?" asked Ray. "You know, deep down, did you realise that something was up? That he spoke the truth?"

"Not at all, mate," answered Guy, smiling. "You see, denial was another friend to me." Ray nodded, satisfied with his answer.

Martha fidgeted in her chair before interjecting. "But, was there *anything* anyone could've said to you to make a difference? You know, to shake you and wake you up?"

"Sadly no, my love. You see, addiction is a mental illness. It's not a rational thing. And so to try and try to make an addict see sense by reasoning with them is just a waste of energy. They can't, and frankly don't want to, see what you see." Martha looked to the floor, crossing her arms and legs in defeat.

"Anyway, things went from bad to worse, and the following year, after a two-week bender, with no recollection of anything, my mum put me in a psychiatric ward. Wanting to please her, I went along for the break, but I fully intended to go on another bender as soon as I came out. That intention kept me going.

"Anyway, around that time, my best mate was due to get married, and knowing all about the hospital admission, he made it very clear that I'd be very welcome at the wedding, so long as I didn't drink. I decided to go, and managed to hold it together, but secretly drank without them knowing. All I could think at that time was 'poor me'. I was completely self-obsessed.

"Then I started seeing another girl. She had a friend who gave me a job. He was a lovely bloke who recognised I had a similar problem to his dad. We spoke about it and I started going to Alcoholics Anonymous with my girlfriend once a week. At this point I wasn't drinking at all.

"So had I turned a corner? Absolutely not! On the outside it appeared that I was in recovery, but in fact, I was only going through the motions to please other people. I wasn't doing it for myself. I was what's known as a 'dry drunk'; a ticking time-bomb waiting to explode.

"A: I didn't want to stop drinking, and B: attending a meeting once a week was no way enough to support my needs. Anyway, I felt that my girlfriend was trying to control me. We had a massive row at Christmas and I drank for a whole week, blacking out. At this point I was placed on suicide watch.

"I pulled myself around again and returned to work, with no one around me, other than my boss, knowing what was going on. But it wasn't long before I went on a four-week-long bender on my own in my flat. Eventually, my dad found me in the bath and called the doctor, who got me in to hospital where I spent the next two weeks healing physically. I can honestly say that at this point, I still didn't think I had a problem.

"A nurse asked me if I wanted a drink, and I said I didn't, so they let me out. It was true that I didn't want to drink at that point, but as soon as I was out of hospital, I got addicted to sex sites instead – anything to fill this void in me. I went six weeks without a drink, and I met a girl online. She was young and mentally screwed up, and so began another cycle; boozing, not turning up to work, letting people down. My parents wanted to section me, but fortunately it never came to that.

"My dad, who in many respects had been responsible for a lot of pain and devastation through my life, had recently met a lady who was a recovering alcoholic, and he put us in touch. He actually came up trumps for once! And it seemed like divine timing. During a long chat with her, something clicked, and I went along to a meeting. I had finally had enough of living like this. This was my awakening point, and I remember driving along three days after the meeting and thinking to myself, 'Do you know what, Guy? Life ain't actually all that bad.'

"But the recovery took time, and I soon fell off the wagon again. I went to a work's event, drank five bottles of wine, drove home completely off my face, and was paranoid that I must've killed someone on route. I lost five days.

"But I returned to regular AA meetings, and took all of the steps in, absorbing them like a sponge and embracing them wholeheartedly. It was the spirituality of these meetings that began to fill my soul. Finally I was doing this for me. It was safe to be myself with these other people who understood completely.

I could leave the ego behind. I had nothing to prove when I was there. But then I had to learn to introduce these steps into my everyday life. They had to become an intrinsic part of who I was, and who I am.

"After a while, I connected with a fella who later became my sponsor; someone I can turn to with any of life's up and downs. Someone who reminds me constantly about looking after myself and retaining healthy and essential boundaries. Someone who was honest enough to tell me I might as well have had 'fuck off' tattooed on my forehead when I first came along to a meeting!

"And you guys are fortunate to have that in Annie. She won't mince her words. Her honesty is the greatest love you'll ever know.

"Anyway, folks, it's been a real pleasure to meet you all. I've got to get off now I'm afraid, as I still attend regular meetings myself, which have to remain my number-one commitment. But please, if you have any questions, or want to discuss anything over the coming week, then don't hesitate to give me a call. I'd be delighted to help if I can."

He wrote his number out on several scraps of paper, ensuring we all had one, and swiftly left the room, throwing his jacket on as he went.

Chapter Fifteen

I poked my head around the pale blue curtain which surrounded Annie's hospital bed. The smell of the ward took me back to the many hours of sitting at my dad's bedside, and my stomach churned with nerves.

Annie's face brightened as I walked towards her and she flung her arms open.

"Hello, my darling," she said, squeezing me tight. "How lovely of you to visit me." Her warm welcome settled me down in an instant.

"Annie, I've been so worried. We all have. I mean, the thought that we could have lost you. Thank heavens you're ok."

"I must admit, I thought my time was up too, darling, but no. He doesn't want me yet; Him upstairs. He reckons I've still got more work to do down here. Quite frankly, I'm exhausted with it all." She chuckled to herself.

"Well, I'm glad He *doesn't* want you. I don't know what we'd all do if you weren't here."

"You'd all do very well, my dear. It's hard sometimes, but we have to accept that all good things come to an end. And when they end, wonderful new things have room to take their place."

"Nothing could replace you, Annie. You're our angel."

We spent some time chatting about general things; Annie telling me all about a wonderful documentary she'd watched last night, and then relaying some funny stories about the various characters on the ward.

I told her a bit about my job and my friendship with Saffie, explaining how difficult it was to watch her struggle, and hoping I might be able to help her out in time.

Annie cleared her throat and peered down her nose intently at me. I could tell she had something serious on her mind. "What is it that you want for yourself, Jude, darling? How do you want your life to be?"

Her words took me by surprise a little, and I mulled over the question. "I guess I just want to be happy. I want to feel good about myself, and to be loved for who I am."

"Now, listen to me carefully, Jude – this is important. I want you to understand that you, my darling, are a powerful creator. You may not believe it, but you are. You have all the tools you need to manifest something amazing; to bring about the life you so want. You just need to direct your focus, believe in yourself and be grateful for everything you have. It's very simple; you just have to believe it.

"And I know you will. I have every faith in you. One hundred percent. Now off you go, darling, I need some sleep. These drugs they're pumping me full of are making me feel ever so queer."

Taking her hand, I stood up and kissed her on the forehead, inwardly smiling at her use of language.

"Hurry up and get yourself well, Annie. We're all missing you. Everyone loves you so much you know."

Smiling, she nodded and closed her eyes.

Chapter Sixteen

As I headed out of my flat for work, my cards caught my eye and beckoned me to interact. With only a minute or two to spare before I missed my bus, I gave them a quick shuffle and asked for some guidance for my day ahead with Saffie.

I picked a card and popped it in my bag, closing the door behind me. It was only when I got on the bus that I looked at it properly. It showed a picture of a bow and arrow, firing at a target, accompanied by the words 'TIME FOR ACTION – you can do it!'

I had a pretty good idea what this was about. It was time to put some ideas to my friend on how I could help her.

"You look rather pleased with yourself this morning, Judith. How was Annie?"

"Annie's doing ok thanks, Saff. She's very tired, but her spirits are good and I think she'll be ok you know."

"That's wonderful, honey. I'm pleased for you." Saffie looked ashen-faced. "Listen, Jude, I think we need to have a chat. I've been sweeping this problem under the carpet for long enough, and it's time I shared it with you."

"Well then, shoot. I'm all ears."

"The thing is, honey, I've finally summoned up the courage and strength to write some figures down, and as I feared, it hasn't made for pretty reading."

"Go on."

"Well, in order for Sol and I to eat well, heat our home and pay the bills, I looks like I'll need to make a really difficult decision. Either I sell the shop and get a permanent part-time job that fits around school hours, or I swallow the rent rise and sever my overheads.

"But whichever choice I make, it's going to have an impact on you, and that's the last thing I ever wanted to happen." Tears welled up in Saffie's eyes. "It's just, however I look at it; whether I turn it inside out or upside down, I'm going to have to let you down in some way."

I rubbed Saffie's arm in a 'there there' motion and smiled. "Saff, you're not letting me down. It's just time for a change that's all. So tell me, sweetheart, what's your preferred option – selling up or not?"

Saffie took a big breath in and let out a huge sigh, seeming relieved at my calmness. "Well, I think all of this has made me realise how much I love the shop. And not just the shop itself, but the customers, the suppliers, and the products too. I still enjoy working here and doing this, Jude.

"But then I think about the flip side you see, and I know full well that I couldn't juggle the shop and Sol's needs without a flexible and reliable member of staff. And there's no one I'd rather work with than you. So I go around in a big circle and can't seem to come to any clear conclusions."

"Well then, allow me to help. Look, Saff, I've been thinking..."

"Sounds dangerous," she winked through her tears.

"...and I have a little idea to put to you. Now, I don't know if it would work or not, but I think it's worth discussing."

Saffie sat up in anticipation, looking hopeful.

"You see, I think we're a bit of a force to be reckoned with, you and me. And I think that Mr Landlord's greed isn't enough to destroy things here."

"Right?"

"And I was thinking about our stock room, and how we might be able to put it to better use."

"Ok? ..."

"Well, I wondered whether we could clear it out and introduce a service. Like a therapy room or something. We could offer readings on one day, massage on another and so on, and open late a couple of evenings a week perhaps. You know, get therapists in, and maybe Rose too."

"Jude, it sounds like a lovely idea and it definitely has some mileage. But these things take time to get going. And I need the money now. Sorry, honey, I don't want to put a dampener on things, but I don't think it's an immediate solution."

"Well that's the bit I was coming too. You see, I've just got a bit of money through from my sister. You know, from Dad. It's not loads, and I need most of it to clear some debts and get straight myself, but it's enough that I don't need to take a wage from you for a few months, and there's more to come when his house is sold."

"Really? Well, how's that going to work then? I can't expect you to work for nothing."

"But maybe you could if I was an investor. Or a partner perhaps?"

Saffie's eyes lit up. "Well there's no one I'd rather share my business with than you, Jude, and it's a lovely thought, but how could it work?"

"Well, that's what we need to decide Saff – explore a few options and see if it's possible."

We sat with our heads together for the rest of the day, brainstorming ideas and whittling them down to the ones that may work financially. Both Saffie and I were buzzing with excitement at the prospect of a brighter future. I was ready for a new challenge, and she was ready for some help.

By closing time, we had a short list of favourite options:-

1. We could shift some stock by holding a heavily discounted Christmas shopping evening, generating some cash and clearing out the stock room at the same time. We were already in the latter stages of November, so this one had to happen straight away. Then future stock could be housed in the kitchen, under the shop counter, and if need be, at Saffie's place.

2. I would focus all my energies on getting the therapy room up and running for the new year. Decorating it, employing therapists, and spreading the word with emails and leaflets. I would take my wage from Dad's winnings, leaving Jude to sort out the rent.

3. I would run the therapy room as my part of the business, and any profits would cover my wages and marketing. I would still work in the shop, being available to manage things when Saffie couldn't be around. And Saffie would still be responsible for paying all of the rent but not have to pay me a wage.

4. We would both pay the rent and share the profits from both sides of the business equally.

We were pretty much agreed on options one and two. We just had to decide how to manage things financially. Things were looking up, and the cards had been right. Two heads were better than one.

Chapter Seventeen

A loud rap at the door woke me with a jump. It was eight-thirty on a Sunday morning; the one day of the week I liked to lie in and catch up on some precious zeds. Perhaps if I ignored it, they would get the hint and disappear.

Giving in to their persistence, I dragged myself up, flung my dressing gown around my shoulders and tentatively opened the door.

"Morning, love. This letter came for you yesterday. It needed signing for, so I signed it on your behalf. Hope that's alright."

Through bleary eyes, I relieved the kind chap from next door of the said envelope, mustering the most gracious smile I could manage given the circumstances, and thanking him as he disappeared back to his flat. Blinking heavily to clear the mist, I realised that the letter was from India. My heart raced madly and my palms started to sweat. Could this be from Matt? It was impossible to tell from the printed label. Kicking the door shut behind me, I decided a coffee was in order before I took the plunge in finding out.

While the kettle was boiling, I picked a card, feeling the need for some kind of support. Three women in a celebratory embrace appeared before me, along with the message: 'SISTERHOOD – friendship is a blessing to be cherished'.

I thumbed open the envelope to find a handwritten letter from Meeta and a photo of her, sitting with Gulab on her garden wall in Patiala, smiling. Breathing a huge sigh of relief, I poured my coffee and began to read.

Hello, dear Jude.

We are so happy to hear from you. We have been worried when we hear you are not returning to Punjab. We want to say sorry for you losing your father. Gulab tells me how hard this is and I find it painful to imagine. And we hear from Matt that you stay with your family in England for now. He tell me you are fine but I feel that this may not be true.

Gulab has missed your visitations. And I miss you every day, especially at yoga class. We are both very happy to hear that you may come back to Patiala to see us again. We think this is wonderful.

It gets cold here now. Nearly winter time. Not like the sunshine you see when you were here! Our winter be very sunny if you come to see us. You know you are always being welcome.

Love and blessings from Patiala.

Your friend, Meeta xxx

Warm tears trickled down my chilly face as I looked at the photo of my two special friends, and I felt a wonderful sense of peace that all was well between us. As soon as Dad's house was sold, I would be there like a shot.

Life seemed pretty good at the moment; much brighter than it had in a long time. Saffie seemed much less stressed, and we both looked forward to our exciting new venture together. Annie was out of hospital and back at home now, with a carer visiting once a day to make her bed and help her get ready until she was strong enough to do it for herself again. And I drew strength every day from the steps we had learnt, which seemed to fit nicely with my cards too. I didn't feel alone, and I felt supported and guided by Pure Love.

There was still one thing that continued to haunt me though, and that was Matt. On the one hand I hated him for what he and Deb had done, but yet another part of me still longed for him. I couldn't imagine ever feeling for anyone else what I'd felt with Matt. My need was overwhelming and I still longed for his touch and yearned for his closeness.

But whenever I got like this, I found it useful to return to the Serenity Prayer, focusing on the acceptance of this situation that

I could not change. It didn't stop the feelings, but it did bring comfort.

Annie had messaged the group to still meet up on Wednesday, and we all arrived to find The Great Raymondo looking particularly jolly. As we made ourselves a cuppa in the kitchen, he needed no prompting.

"I found out on Monday that my job is safe!"

"Oh, nice one, mate," replied Shane the Mane, his shaggy hair hanging loose around his face.

"I felt really bad for my colleague at the time who's lost his job, but it turns out that he was hoping for the redundancy anyway. I can't tell you how relieved I am, and I even found myself telling Maria about it. I think it's really helped you know."

"Ray, that's great news," I added, patting him on the arm.

"So, this is what you all do when Annie's not here then is it?" came a voice from the kitchen door. "Stand around drinking tea and chatting?" It was Guy, grinning cheekily.

We walked through to the main room and grabbed a chair each (a job that Annie usually did for us), and arranged them in a circle.

Guy, who had subsequently made himself a coffee, was last to sit down. "Right then, folks. I'll be here for the duration this evening. I managed to get to an AA meeting last night, so I won't have to rush off this time.

"Now, Annie has asked that we discuss Step Eleven together, and then she would like Jude to take over the running of this evening's meeting."

"Hey? Why would Annie want me to do that? I don't know enough about it," I asked, feeling my cheeks blush with surprise and embarrassment.

Guy smiled. "Well, I don't know, Jude, but I'm sure Annie does. Let's just trust her, eh?"

"Well, ok then," I agreed

"So then, folks, Step Eleven: *We seek through prayer and*

meditation to improve our conscious contact with God (whatever our understanding of that may be), praying only for knowledge of His will for us, and the power to carry that out."

We all took a while to absorb the words and their meaning.

Shane scratched his head, looking puzzled. "I've kind of got my head around the prayer bit, but I must admit, I'm a bit lost on the meditation front. If we're being asked to meditate on our own, then I'm not really sure what I'm supposed to do."

For once, I felt able to help. "Well, my understanding of meditation, from my time in India, is that you take time to relax and focus on something specific. So my interpretation of this step is that we take time out to sit quietly and ask for guidance from our God."

I looked to Guy who was nodding approvingly. "Do you still meditate, Jude?"

"Well, to be honest, I seriously lost my way when I came back to the UK. My situation got really difficult and I fell apart. But looking back now with what I've learnt from Annie and this group, I didn't need to feel quite so alone, and things didn't need to be quite so bad."

Raymondo chipped in, "But don't you think things *had* to get really bad in order for Annie to find us and share her knowledge of these steps?"

"Ray, you're totally right, mate," agreed Shane. "I would've laughed about all this stuff a while back. I would have called it mumbo jumbo. But now it just makes sense."

Mousey Martha, who had been pretty quiet up until now, chipped in with her views too. "Well, I pray every day; always have done. But thinking about this step, I guess I've always prayed for things to be different, and for my son to change, rather than focusing on what *I* can do."

"Interesting isn't it?" added Guy.

We continued to chat about how the steps were helping our individual situations, and before I knew it, it was time for the session to end. I realised that although I'd been instructed to lead the meeting, it had pretty much taken care of itself. Perhaps to share my understanding of meditation was all that was needed.

"Get yourselves home safely, folks. I'll give group leader Jude, a hand to put the chairs away." Guy winked, teasing me for being the chosen one, albeit kindly.

We stacked the chairs and I washed up my mug. I looked at my watch, and realising I'd missed my bus anyway, I flicked the kettle back on. "Would you like a tea or coffee, Guy? I've got thirty minutes to kill."

"Oh, go on then, I'll have a coffee. Milk no sugar please."

"So, what is it that you do for a day job, Guy?"

"I'm a graphic designer. How about you?"

"Oh, I work in a gift shop in town, 'The Treasure Chest'. It's my friend's shop, but we've decided to go into partnership. We're in the process of revamping and relaunching, so there's loads to organise – converting a room, hiring different services, and getting the word out there."

"That sounds exciting! Well, give me a shout if you need any help. I'm a dab hand with a paintbrush you know."

"Well, that's really kind of you. I'll certainly bear that in mind and might even hold you to it! Come to think of it, I *do* need some leaflets making up. Don't suppose you could design something for me? I'll pay you of course."

"Yeah, no worries. Just send over the logo and wording and I'll get some ideas to you next week. I can't do it for nothing I'm afraid. It's a promise I made to myself a long time ago you see. But I can certainly give you a favourable rate and I'm sure you won't be disappointed."

"Brilliant, thanks! Well, that's one less thing to worry about then. And I wouldn't expect you to do it for nothing by the way. It's your job."

"I'll gladly give you a couple of hours of my time for painting though if you need the manpower. No charge for that one. Only for my day job." Guy winked.

"Well thank you. I'm really glad I missed my bus now! Speaking of which, I'd best not miss my next one. I'll be in touch."

We said our farewells and headed off in opposite directions. What a nice chap, I thought. It seemed more apparent than ever that friendship, be it old or new, was a gift to be truly treasured.

Chapter Eighteen

I was so excited about our plans for the shop and how good it could be, but there was so much to be done that I didn't know quite where to start. I wanted to secure a handful of different services to offer our customers, but so far I hadn't much clue about what, who or how. Feeling overwhelmed by it all, I shuffled my deck and picked a card for guidance.

I was shown a picture of a girl with a knife pointing at her head. No one seemed to be holding the knife, and neither was it close enough to hurt her. 'UNFOUNDED FEARS – it's time to confront them' was the message.

Ok, ok, I thought. I had to start somewhere, so I would begin by calling Rose. I still had her number, and fortunately she was in and had time to chat.

"Rose, it's Jude from The Treasure Chest. Do you remember me? You kindly gave me a reading."

"Oh hello, dear. How are you getting on with your cards?"

"I absolutely love them, Rose. They seem to comfort and guide me. Thanks so much for bringing them in, it was really kind of you."

"It's a pleasure, dear. And thank *you* for putting the poster up for me. I've had a few calls you know. You can't beat a nice exchange."

"Well, that's brilliant news!" I replied. "Anyway, the reason for my call is that I've decided to go into partnership with my friend, Saffie, who owns the shop. We're in the process of clearing out our stock room and transforming it into a therapy room. We want to offer various services to our customers, and you're my first port of call. I wondered if you'd like to work from the shop one day a week, giving readings?"

"Oh, and you thought of me? How lovely. Well, dear, the idea sounds marvellous in theory. But the only day I have free at the moment is a Thursday."

"Well, that's fine with me, Rose, as you're the first person I've called. So can I pencil you in for Thursdays then? We'll start up in the new year, but I'll let you have the finer details nearer the time."

"Why not? Let's do it!" Rose chuckled.

"Great! Now to find five other people who want to work with us too! Don't suppose you know anyone who might be interested do you?"

"Errrr. Well I do know that my friend Shona is looking for a new clinic to practice from. She's an acupuncturist. Might be worth calling her to see if she's interested? And then there's Toni who does spiritual healing. Lovely lady. She travels far and wide to do her work, and might be glad of a base that's closer to home."

"Oh, fabulous. Thanks, Rose, I'll definitely call them."

Rose gave me their details, and slowly, The Treasure Chest's new 'box of delights' began to fill up. It made me realise that sometimes all you need to do is make a start, and the rest will fall into place.

Later that day, Annie sent each of the group a message, asking us to meet at hers this week. I *did* wonder whether it would be too much for her, but she seemed pretty adamant that that's what she wanted. And when Annie's mind was made up, there was no point in trying to change it. Besides, none of us would dare to try anyway.

We arrived at her bungalow; a small but pretty cream building with a stained-glass picture of an owl on the front door. There were flowers everywhere, and the place felt well-loved. We piled into Annie's tiny front room, much to her delight at having some dearly wanted company. Despite her ill health, she remained dressed up to the nines in brightness, with sparkly jewellery and plenty of rouge.

Everyone bent down to kiss her cheek as they entered the

room, relaying their fears about her health problems.

"It's so wonderful to see you all, darlings, and thank you for coming to me this time. It's lovely to know how much you care, but did you honestly think I was going to croak it before I've taught you the full twelve steps for goodness sake?!" She winked and licked her lips cheekily.

"Now then, how are we all doing? Martha, let's start with you, darling."

Something about Mousey Martha had changed this week. Aside from her new haircut and bright red bag, she actually looked quite relaxed, and less, well....mousey.

"Do you know, Annie, I feel like I'm finally making some progress – as if I've turned a bit of a corner. The situation with my son hasn't changed; that's still upsetting and stressful, but I think I'm learning to focus a bit more on me and *my* happiness now. Something seems to have shifted, and I feel as though I'm actually *conversing* with God for the first time, and that some of the guilt and shame that I've carried around for all these years has left me."

"Well that's wonderful, darling. Keep returning to the steps and you'll continue to find strength – like I still do every day." Everyone smiled as though we were all genuinely pleased for Martha.

"Shane? How about you, darling? How are you getting on?"

"Well, since I last saw you – you know, when I'd had that relapse for want of a better word – I feel like the meanings of the steps are really starting to sink in and make sense. I must admit, I *did* struggle with the whole God thing to start with, as I'd had a problem with this God bloke who'd taken my mum away from me. But now I've found a way to *make* Mum my God, well that's changed everything. It all makes sense and I take great comfort in feeling close to her again. She always loved and supported me, and I feel like she's able to do that again. And, Annie, I want to thank you from the bottom of my heart for helping me to find that reassurance."

Shane the Mane was having to look up at the ceiling to stop his tears from rolling down his face. It was heart-warming to see him so attuned to his emotions. Chest hair aside, there was no sign of bravado or machismo about him this week. Martha handed him a tissue and patted him on the back of his hand; an action that took Annie by surprise. She smiled lovingly at them, seeing that they had forgiven their differences somewhere along the way.

"And how about you, Ray, my darling?"

The Great Raymondo's cheeks were rosier than ever. Mind you, Annie's room was mightily warm. He too looked quite relaxed; less nervy than usual.

"Well, I'm pleased to say, Annie, that I managed to keep my job, and have since confided in Maria. I've been praying every day this week for the power to carry out God's wishes for me, and have drawn great strength from that. And do you know what? We are starting to talk a bit more. Not small talk, but about stuff that *really* matters.

"And like Shane said, I feel supported. Alright, I know the debts are still there. None of that's gone away. But I somehow know that I will deal with this, and it'll be ok. Deep down I know we'll have to sell our house at some point and downsize. But hopefully, when the time's right, I'll find the right words to put this to Maria."

Annie nodded in agreement. "Well, my goodness, darlings, it *has* been a positive week. Now don't forget, it won't always feel like this. But rest assured you'll have all the tools you need to get you through. You just have to remember to use them!" Annie winked. "And how's this week been for you, Jude?"

I told Annie and the group about my plans with Saffie for the shop, and how, with the help of the steps and my spiritual cards, solutions were starting to present themselves to me. I invited everyone in the group to our Christmas shopping bargain event, and they all seemed keen to support me. Annie promised to write me a shopping list of presents that she needed for her nieces, nephews and grandchildren, and asked me to source them from The Treasure Chest. "It'll be a weight off my mind, darling," she explained.

We looked together at Step Twelve – our final step in the programme: *Having had a spiritual awakening as a result of these steps, we try to carry this message to others, and to practice these principles in all our affairs.*

I thought about Annie. And Guy too. They were both living proof that the steps *could* restore you to sanity, if you focused on your problems one day at a time. And what's more, they weren't afraid to get themselves out there and share this message. Not to just anyone, but to those who seemed ready to listen and hear; to people who desperately needed their love and support. They went wherever they felt guided; like angels I thought. I sat for a while in admiration, and hoped that one day I too could be such a loving role model.

Chapter Nineteen

I arrived at The Treasure Chest to find Guy waiting for me at the door.

"What time do you call this then?" he joked. "Thought you'd at least have the kettle on by now!"

I checked my watch and winked. "I call this on time actually, Guy."

I'd made sure I wasn't late for our meeting. Guy was bringing in some design ideas for the leaflets and he'd offered to give me a hand with the painting while he was there. It was Sunday, so the shop was officially closed. Just as well, I thought. There was mess everywhere.

Saffie was due in shortly to sort through the boxes of stock; what was going into our sale, what was being stored in the shop, and what she'd be taking home. And my job was to freshen up our new therapy room which we now fondly referred to as The Box of Delights.

"Nice to see you made an effort," Guy said, teasing me about my paint-stained jeans and old polo shirt which I'd ruined whilst painting my flat.

"Hey! What are you saying? This is my Sunday best I'll have you know."

Guy laid out three different design options. They were all good, but one in particular stood out as perfect.

"Hey, Saff, this is Guy. What do you think of his leaflet designs?"

Saffie took a large bite of buttered toast she'd grabbed from the coffee shop, waved the rest of the slice at Guy, and peered over the counter. "Ooh, I'm loving *that* one."

"Me too," I chuckled. "Glad we both agree. Looks like this is the outright winner then."

"I had a feeling it would be," replied Guy. "I'll get a load run off for you in the next couple of days. Nothing like a last-minute panic to put a rocket up your arse, eh?" Guy had been really helpful in turning the leaflets around so quickly. Fair enough, I was paying for them, but he had bent over backwards nevertheless.

"Thanks, Guy. I owe you one."

"No worries. Might have to go and get myself some toast before we start. Smells delish. Either of you want anything while I'm there?"

"No thanks," we replied.

As soon as he was out of earshot, Saffie nudged me hard in the arm. "So, come on then? Spill the beans. What's with you and Mr Nice Guy then? Get it? Mr Nice *Guy*?"

"Yes, I get it. Hilarious."

"Well?"

"Well nothing. There's nothing to spill. He's just a friendly and helpful chap who's offered to give me a hand."

"And how are you going to repay him, dear Judith? He must want something in return," she teased, scanning me up and down.

"Honestly, Saff, it's not like that."

"Why, has he got a girlfriend then? You'd make a cute little match you know."

"I don't know if he has a girlfriend or not ,Saff, and I'm really not interested. He's just a nice bloke that's all."

"Ok, ok. If you say so."

"I do. So let it go now please?"

Guy walked back in. "Right then, refuelled and ready for action ladies!"

Saffie nudged her foot into mine under the counter. Ignoring her, I pointed to the old stock room. "This way then. Let the painting commence."

The three of us worked well together and the morning passed really quickly. Guy freshened up the ceiling and did all the high bits, while I did the crouching down bits that caused my thighs to feel like jelly. We opted to keep things simple, white and clean-looking. I had a couple of nice paintings of brightly coloured angels at home which I'd done years ago. They'd fit the theme of the room perfectly, I thought.

Guy disappeared at midday to get started on the printing of the leaflets. If we had them by Tuesday, we could start putting the word out straight away. There was no time to lose. Our Christmas shopping evening was next Saturday and I hoped to be able to tell everyone about the treatments we had planned for the new year. I still had a couple of therapists to find but didn't know quite where to seek them as yet.

Saffie had worked hard on the display, with one side of the shop dedicated to our full-priced items, and the other half chocked full of reduced bargains. We'd decided to be bold and offer our Christmas shoppers below-cost-price deals, focusing on how they were helping to clear our stock room rather than what Saffie may have lost along the way. If all went well then we'd probably keep a bargain corner going to entice people in from the street.

Our finishing touch was the huge Christmas tree in the corner, which we tastefully decorated with traditional red and gold beads and bows, whilst singing along to our favourite carols and sampling the mulled wine that we'd be handing out to our guests. Whoever would have thought that this amount of hard work could be so much fun?

Guy, bless him, not only stuck to his promise of getting the leaflets to us by Tuesday, he turned up with them at close of business on Monday instead. Saffie had already left to pick Sol up from rugby practice and I was about to lock up.

"Oh wow! Guy, you're a star. I really can't thank you enough for everything you've done." Without thinking, I picked up a bottle of mulled wine to give to him as a gesture, and then blushed profusely as I remembered his drink problem.

"You trying to push me off the wagon or something?" His cheeky smile put me at ease and I admired how accepting he was of his situation.

"Honestly, my brain at times. I'm sorry, Guy. Tell you what, I'm locking up now. Fancy grabbing a quick pizza if you're not busy? My treat."

"Well, that does sound tempting, Jude. Only I'm not sure what her indoors would think if I ate dinner with someone else."

"Oh, sorry. I didn't mean anything by it. I just wanted to say thanks, that's all."

Guy grinned again. "I'm only teasing you, Jude. Her indoors is my cat Phoebe. She expects her dinner to be served bang on six pm. But I guess I can make an exception this once and deal with her sulks later. She's a demanding little minx you know!"

We laughed. "Seriously though, pizza would be lovely. Thank you."

Spending time with Guy was easy. We chatted about Annie, the shop, the twelve steps and my cards, and before we knew it, the waiters were turning the lights out. I paid the bill and Guy walked me to the bus stop.

"So how's the meditation going now, Jude? Do you feel like you're getting your spirituality back on track again?"

"It's definitely getting easier, but I'm still not at peace like I was in Punjab. I'm hoping to get over there again for a visit soon. I miss my lovely friends."

"Well I know it's not exactly on the same level as India, but I go to a really nice meditation class on a Thursday evening at a unit down on the farm. You're welcome to come along. I think you'd really like the lady who runs it."

"Ooh, that sounds nice. Thursdays are always pretty quiet in the shop, so I can always get away on time. It'd be nice to meditate with others again. What time?"

"It starts at seven-thirty. I could pick you up just after seven if you like? I've got to come past you anyway."

The bus pulled in to the stop and I jumped on. "Sounds perfect. Thanks, Guy. I'll look forward to that." He waved and we headed off home.

For the next few days, Saffie and I made great progress, handing out our leaflets to customers and placing bundles of them in various local shops. We also sent the artwork to the editor of our local free magazine who promised to get it into this week's issue.

Before I knew it, Thursday evening had arrived, and I was deliberating over what to wear to the meditation group. I plaited my hair to the side in case I'd be lying down, and settled on some leggings and a long-sleeved indigo kaftan with the 'om' symbol swirled on the front. I popped some woolly socks in my bag, along with a bottle of water, and threw a heavy shawl around my shoulders, hoping I'd be warm enough.

The unit was only ten minutes drive from me which meant that we arrived a little early. A rickety old door led us through to a bright airy room with a high beamed ceiling.

"Oh look, that's Yogi Bhajan," I said to Guy, pointing at a poster on the wall of a bearded man in a white turban.

"Yogi who?"

"Bhajan. He was a wonderful Sikh man who taught kundalini yoga and brought it over to the West. He showed people around the world how they didn't need drugs to experience a state of higher consciousness. They could achieve it through this form of yoga. He set up drug rehab centres around the globe."

"Oh wow! He sounds like a legend."

"Yes. My Sikh friends in Punjab said he was not only humble, but fearlessly outspoken. A formidable teacher by all accounts."

"A wonderful man!" came a gentle voice from the doorway.

"Jude, this is Grace, our meditation teacher. Grace, this is Jude." Grace was dressed from head to toe in white, her braided blonde hair tied loosely back from her pretty, kind face, and her bold green and pink mandala necklace jumping out from all of the whiteness.

"Lovely to meet you, Grace. I used to go to a kundalini yoga class in Punjab. Bit far to travel now though."

Grace smiled. "Well, if ever you're looking for a new class, I teach one here on a Saturday morning."

"Oh, what a shame. I work on Saturdays."

Other students began to trickle in and take their seats – some on chairs, some on cushions and some on meditation stools. The evening was lovely and I revelled in the feeling of oneness. But although I enjoyed the peace and tranquillity of the silent session, I kept feeling frustrated that I'd been led to this beautiful lady who taught kundalini yoga and yet I couldn't attend her class. Towards the end of the session, a thought popped into my mind. Maybe Grace could bring her teachings to the shop.

Putting all fears to the back of my mind, I hung back and approached her as she was clearing away.

"Lovely session thanks, Grace. I really enjoyed myself."

"Oh, I'm glad, and it's a pleasure to have you here."

"I was just wondering if you'd be interested in getting involved with a new therapy room we're opening in The Treasure Chest? It's quite a small room, so I guess it wouldn't be much use for group work, but you could do one-to-one sessions in there or use the main shop floor when we're closed in the evenings."

"Well that's so funny," Grace said smiling. "I've been asking the gods to guide me towards a space where I can practice my massage. I don't suppose that could work for you could it?"

"I think that could actually work very nicely indeed. I was a bit nervous about asking you."

"Well I'm very glad you did. How about I call into the shop and have a look at the space? If it's viable to hold a class there and we can drum up the interest then all the better, but I'll need you to provide a few mats and cushions if that's ok?"

"Sounds great! I'm in there most days, so please do pop in. Oh, and if you're interested, we're having a Christmas shopping evening on Saturday night. Heavily reduced gift ideas and a glass of mulled wine too."

"Well, how can I refuse? I'll see you then, Jude. And thanks again."

As I slipped into bed that evening, I felt a huge sense of gratitude for how things seemed to be falling into place. I thanked Pure Love for supporting me, before drifting off into the most wonderful sleep.

Chapter Twenty

It was the day before the Christmas shopping event and young Sol was helping Saffie to clear out the last of the mess in the shop, leaving me free to pop round to Annie's to get her shopping list.

She seemed so pleased to see me, as I was her, and I went into the kitchen to make us both a cup of tea.

"Do you take sugar, Annie?"

"I like to think I'm sweet enough thanks, darling, but I *will* have a sweetener. Now then, I like my cup to be two thirds full and only a dash of milk." She gave a little chuckle, knowing full well how fussy she was. I admired her ability to communicate her needs so clearly and lovingly to get what she wanted. "And there are some biscuits in that tin up there if you can reach. Help yourself to what you want."

I popped her porcelain mug down beside her. "How are you feeling today?"

"Well, darling, I *have* felt better, but I must accept that this is how things are for now, and keep reminding myself that *this too shall pass*." She took a big gulp of tea. "Ooh, that's lovely. So, come on then, let's talk about this shopping list."

I explained the kind of things we sold, and Annie told me about her friends and family and the sort of things they'd like. As she leant forward to place her mug back down on the table, she winced.

"Ooh, are you ok?"

"Oh, it's nothing, darling. Just my feet are so dry that my socks keep catching every now and then, and I can't bend down far enough to reach them at the moment."

"Would you like me to rub some cream in for you?"

Annie's eyes filled with tears. "Oh would you, darling? Oh that's ever so kind."

"Really, it's nothing." I massaged her feet and we chatted

about what I'd been up to lately.

"Well, it seems as though you've been seeing quite a bit of my lovely Guy." Annie winked.

"Oh, not you as well," I laughed. "My friend Saffie keeps teasing me about that, but honestly, nothing has happened between Guy and me. He's such a nice man and we do get on really well, but we're just friends."

Annie stared down at me. "You must admit though, Jude, he *is* rather gorgeous." A smile crept over her face, "And you would make rather a lovely little couple."

"Well, I don't think he's interested like that anyway, Annie. He certainly hasn't made any advances. We get on really well as friends and that's fine with me."

"Hmmm, well I've known Guy for a long time now, and I can tell you that since he's been in recovery, he's never had a girlfriend."

"Well maybe he likes it that way?"

"Or maybe he's afraid of interfering with *your* recovery. Now I know it's none of my business really, darling, but I *do* keep getting a feeling about you two; and I must say, it's a good one."

"Well, I'll bear that in mind then thanks, Annie." I patted her feet and pulled her fluffy socks back on. "Anyway, I must get going now. It's going to be a looooong day tomorrow."

She opened her arms for a hug. "I hope it goes really well for you, darling. You deserve it, you really do."

As I left Annie's bungalow, a message flashed up on my phone. It was from Deb.

'Hi Jude. Cash buyer came through for Dad's house. Wants to move quickly and has been pushing for a fast exchange which is due to happen on Monday. Looks like the sale will be complete by the end of next week. Please forward your account details and I'll ask the solicitor to pay your half directly to you. Hope you got the cheque I sent you. Deb xx'

A mix of different emotions washed over me all at once; anger with Deb for what she'd done with Matt, sadness at the physical loss of Dad's home, and relief to know that I would soon have the financial freedom to do some wonderful things that Dad would be proud of.

I sobbed and sobbed and sobbed, and not knowing what else to do, I knocked on Annie's door. She held me tightly and stroked my hair gently as I relayed my feelings. "That's it, darling. Let it go. You're perfectly safe. Let it go and it will pass."

It was as if I was she was meant to be there with me when I crumbled, and I thanked Pure Love for my angel, Annie.

By the time I got home that evening I felt much calmer. Deciding to focus my energies on the positives, rather than the negatives, I spent the next two hours booking my flight to Punjab.

Chapter Twenty-One

I awoke to find that the emotional cloud had lifted. My head felt clear, my heart felt open, and I spent plenty of time getting ready for the long day ahead. I showered in my favourite rose gel and applied lashings of orange-and-geranium body butter to my skin.

Leaving that to soak in, I took time applying my makeup and I carefully blow dried my hair into loose curls. Feeling fabulous, I put on a beautiful long-sleeved 'kameez' tunic that I'd bought at the bazaar with Meeta. It was jade green and gold and fitted where it touched, and I teamed it with opaque black tights, suede black ankle boots and a thick gold bangle. I popped a scarlet red lipstick into my bag for later.

Right, all ready to play hostess, I thought. I picked a card for my day ahead. 'NEW BEGINNINGS' was my message, which felt wholly appropriate.

As soon as I arrived at the shop, I loaded a bag up with goodies for Annie and hoped she'd be pleased with the best pick of the bargains. Scented candles, pretty photo frames, skinny scarves, beaded trinket boxes and crystal key rings made up the selection, all of which I'd have been very happy to receive.

A combination of Christmas tunes and further plans for the therapy room made the day pass by in a flash, and before we knew it, customers were arriving in their droves for our event. The atmosphere was buzzing, the till was ringing and everyone seemed to have a fun time. Raymondo and his wife Maria turned up, as did Martha and her friend Hattie. Guy showed his face in support and said how amazing I looked, and Grace came along too. She committed to offering a day per week of massage in the shop and mentioned again about the cushions and mats should there be a demand for meditation or yoga.

Feeling chuffed to bits with the success of our evening, we

cashed up and began to count the monetary value of our efforts. Not only had we shifted loads of bargain stock, but quite a lot of full-priced items too.

"You might as well finish this off, Jude," Saffie said, emptying the remainders of the mulled wine into my mug. "I'll run you home tonight."

Why not, I thought. I hadn't touched a drop all night in order to keep a professional clear head. "Thanks, my lovely. Oh, Saff, I've got something to tell you. Well, a couple of things actually."

"Let me guess, you're seeing Guy?"

"Behave! Guy's just a friend. Honestly, Saff, what are you like? No, what I wanted to tell you is that my dad's house sale is going through and I should get my half of the money next week."

"Oh, wow! That was quick. How do you feel about it, honey?"

"Well, last night I felt really down. It all seemed really final and sad. But once I'd let that go, I was able to focus on the freedom it would give me. You know, as if Dad's still helping me. And one thing I promised myself was to visit Meeta and Gulab as soon as I could afford to. I left them all in such a hurry and pretty much cut them out when they'd been so good to me."

"Right?"

"So, last night, I went ahead and booked a flight out there. I figured that if I went before Christmas, it wouldn't impact too much on our January relaunch. Anyway, I've booked it for next Thursday. I'm sorry it's short notice, but I'll only stay a few days and I'll fly back on the following Monday night. Is that ok?"

"Jude, you haven't taken any time off in months. Of course it's ok on that front. But what about the whole Matt thing? Alarm bells *are* ringing rather loudly in my head at the moment if I'm honest."

"Yeah....well...I haven't thought too much about that one. Only that I wasn't planning to let him know I was going. I just feel I need to spend some time with the two ladies who made me feel so welcome. I owe them that, and I want to give them a hug.

Plus, I thought I could spend some time in the bazaar to see what I could bring back for the shop."

"Well, that all sounds great, but you'd better not bloody well get back with that arsehole, and you'd better come back to me!"

"Of course I'll be back, Saff. I'm not going to let anything get in the way of our plans. The Treasure Chest and it's Box of Delights are our future, and I want this to work as much as you do. Now give me a hug. And a high five for a wonderful evening. To us!"

"To us!" We clinked our mugs together in the air; sisters united.

* * *

I enjoyed a very long lie in the following morning, before calling Annie to arrange a visit. I wanted to pop her bag of goodies round, and also let her know that I wouldn't make this Wednesday's meeting as I had a very early flight to catch the next day.

"Have a wonderful time, darling. And don't get up to anything that I can't, will you? Or I shall be most jealous!" she giggled.

I messaged Guy to let him know that I'd be missing meditation this week, and to thank him for his support over the past couple of weeks.

And then I spent the rest of my Sunday booking a room in Patiala. I'd deliberated over whether to stay with Meeta or not, and although I knew I'd be very welcome, I didn't want to put Prakash in an awkward position with Matt. Difficult though it was, I decided to not even tell Meeta I was coming until the day before.

My journey to Patiala was a long one, and it seemed very odd to arrive in India and still be needing winter woollies. I was delighted to see Meeta's friendly face waiting for me at the train station. We threw our arms around each other and jumped in a cab. She told me I was looking too thin and I explained that life was gradually becoming less stressful and so I was starting to enjoy my food again.

"You are very silly staying in a room that you must pay for, Jude. You should come and stay with Prakash and me."

"That's so kind of you, Meeta, and I know I'd be welcome, but I didn't want Prakash feeling awkward. He has to work with Matt after all."

"Does Matt know you are coming here?"

"No, he doesn't. I've come to spend time with you and Gulab, not Matt. I still miss him, Meeta, but he really hurt me." I was keen to change the subject, not wanting to involve my friend in the nitty gritty of the horridness. "Anyway, enough of all that; tell me what's been happening here."

"Well, Jude, I have some news for you, and I'm so happy you come here so I can tell you. Prakash and me are going to have a baby. It's still very early but if the pregnancy goes well, the baby will come in July."

I took Meeta's hand. "Oh, Meeta. That's wonderful! Congratulations! Are you feeling ok?"

"Yes, thank you. I feel good but I don't want to drink any chai!"

"Crikey! That will never do!" We giggled. "Does Gulab know I've come back?"

"No, she doesn't. I think it's nice to have a surprise for her. She will be so pleased that you are here. We see her in the morning. Are you hungry?"

"I'm *really* hungry. And do you know what I fancy? A stuffed paratha from the bazaar." Meeta chuckled and asked the taxi driver to stop at the food stall.

Freshly baked flatbread, nothing could compare. "It's good to be back," I said, biting into the comforting deliciousness.

They dropped me off to my tiny room which was tired but

clean and warm. I didn't plan on spending much time there so it was absolutely fine. "I come for you at ten o'clock tomorrow, Jude. We can go and surprise Gulab."

"I can't wait to see her!"

"Sleep well. Until tomorrow, my friend."

"Until tomorrow, my pregnant friend." Meeta smiled and jumped back in her cab.

She looked so happy, I thought. Had things been different, I might have been pregnant by now too, and Meeta and I could've enjoyed the beginnings of motherhood together.

Determined to feel awake and refreshed for the day ahead, I crashed in my bed, trying to ignore the fact it was only mid afternoon back in the UK. I felt very conscious that Matt wasn't lying here next to me, but I pushed that to one side, made a mental list of all the things I'd like to buy for the shop and my therapy room, and said the Serenity Prayer.

Please, Pure Love, grant me...
the serenity to accept the things I cannot change,
the courage to change the things I can,
and the wisdom to know the difference.

I couldn't do anything to change the past, but I could do something about the future. And with Saffie, Annie, Meeta, Gulab, Guy, and the twelve steps in my life, not to mention a helpful boost from my loving dad, the future was looking really bright. Focusing on gratitude, I drifted into a lovely sleep.

It felt really odd waking up to a chilly room in Patiala. Still very early, I got dressed straight away, made myself a hot tea, and spent some time by the window, watching the world emerge. Having opted for just a room rather than bed and breakfast, I munched on a cereal bar and looked forward to something tasty at Gulab's. She always had a stash of homemade goodies in her cupboard.

I had brought my faithful cards with me and decided to pick one for the day ahead. As I shuffled the deck, one card slid out, so I chose to go with it, even though I had no clue what it meant. The message was 'CONSEQUENCES – make wise loving choices'. I couldn't see how that was appropriate to the time I had planned with my friends, but I was grateful anyway.

As promised, Meeta arrived at ten am on the dot, wearing a big white smile. "I'm so excited for today, Jude. It's so good to have you here again."

"It's great to see you too, Meeta. How are you feeling this morning?"

"I feel fine thanks."

"Does Gulab know about the pregnancy?"

"She guessed, Jude, when I say no to chai and chai cake!" We laughed. "Let us go to see her now. She is expecting *me* to come, but not you."

Although it was cold, the sky was clear and bright, and we walked arm in arm along the street, plotting our surprise.

"I go in first, Jude, and then after one minute, you knock on the door, ok?"

As planned, I gave a firm knock and Gulab told Meeta to open the door. As I walked in, Gulab was pouring a nutritious glass of Lassi for her pregnant friend. "I hope you have enough for me too," I teased.

Gulab dropped her spoon and walked towards me with open arms. Her hug was so tight, I feared my ribcage would shatter. She jabbered away in Punjabi, put her hands to her heart, and then pointed to the card I'd sent her, which took pride of place on the kitchen dresser.

She took my coat and summoned me to sit down on a stool next to Meeta. The three of us had never been together before, and it felt wonderful. Still speaking Punjabi in a very shrill tone, Gulab pulled various tubs out of her cupboards and removed the lids for me to see what was on offer. "Please, you have some. Very nice." She placed a plate in front of me and encouraged me to dive in.

We enjoyed a cup of chai together, and I had an enormous slab of cake. Meeta suggested we take some lunch to the Sheesh Mahal, a palace I had wanted to visit when I was here before, but had never got around to. Gulab seemed pleased with the idea, and went about packing up a picnic feast.

A taxi dropped us outside the palace, which greeted us with its vision of tranquil beauty. The ladies found a pretty spot to sit and eat beside the lake. Gulab placed a blanket on the bench, to remove the chill from our bottoms, and another blanket across our knees, and we sat there for a good couple of hours, chatting, munching, and sipping hot drinks from our flasks. It was true that the simple things in life really did give the most pleasure.

Horrified at the thought of me sleeping in a little room on my own, Gulab insisted I stay at her place that night, and so our return taxi waited outside while I collected a few things. He dropped Gulab and I back at hers, before taking Meeta home to cook for her husband.

"I meet you here at ten o'clock tomorrow, Jude, and we go shopping. Prakash say you must come back with me for dinner and to stay. He wants to say hello. Please say you will come."

"I'd love to, Meeta. Thank you. See you in the morning."

Later that evening, I received a message on my phone to say that Dad's house had completed and that the money had been transferred over to my account.

"Thanks, Dad," I said, looking up at the sky. Amounts of money aside, it felt wonderful to know that my dad was able to help me, and that he could now be involved in my journey forwards. I felt a little door in my heart, which had closed in sadness when he passed, begin to reopen, and I shed a few tears of joy.

That evening, I relayed the story of Dad's illness and passing to Gulab, who had also lost her father a few years ago, and we shared in the memories of our loved ones. She explained the Sikh tradition of celebrating the lives of their loved ones one year after their death, which I thought was a really lovely idea, and one I would bear in mind.

Whilst Gulab carried out her evening prayer ritual, I spent some time reading a book that Annie had leant me, and it wasn't long before I nodded off in my warm comfortable bed. This wonderful woman was certainly a welcoming hostess, and destined for Heaven, I reckoned.

She greeted me the following morning with a breakfast fit for a queen.

"Wow, Gulab, this looks amazing. You must've got up very early."

"I get up at five hours every morning for prayer." Understanding she meant five o'clock, I nodded and sat down to our feast of spiced Lassi, freshly cooked Parathas stuffed with warm bananas and sugar, peppermint tea, and her famous Chai Masala cake. I told Gulab about my plans for the shop, and she recommended several bazaar stalls to visit for the best bargains, writing their names down on a scrap of paper for me.

Meeta and I had a wonderful day together, and we successfully sourced all of the items on my list. My friend's local knowledge was invaluable when it came to bartering, and we ended up paying impressively low prices that Saffie would not have been able to achieve from the UK. I had filled a large case to its maximum capacity and had arranged for a selection of yoga mats and meditation stools to be shipped over. It felt empowering to know that I had some money in the bank to support me now, and that our shop would be further enhanced by these authentic Indian items of beauty.

I couldn't have felt more welcome in their home that evening, and we celebrated Meeta's pregnancy and my plans for the shop with a beautiful meal. Exciting times lay ahead for us all, and we flopped down on the comfortable sofas with a hot milky bedtime drink.

An unexpected knock on the door made us jump, and Prakash got up to answer it, only to find Matt standing there. My heart almost leapt out of my chest and I didn't know what to do. Feeling obviously awkward, Prakash tried to get rid of him.

"Matt, my friend, I told you not to come here tonight."

"I know, and I'm sorry, but I need to see my wife." Ignoring Prakash's polite pleas, he walked through the door, and towards me. "Jude, we need to talk. Why didn't you tell me you were coming?"

Prakash blushed and looked apologetically at me. "Jude, I'm so sorry. I couldn't lie to my friend, but I did explain you didn't want to see him."

Feeling shaky, I turned to Matt. "Ok, let's talk. I'll meet you tomorrow."

"How about we talk now, Jude? For all I know you'll be gone tomorrow."

I grabbed my coat, kissed Meeta on the cheek and headed towards the door. "Fine. But not here. This is our friends' home."

"Let's get a cab back to our place. I mean, my place." Matt hailed a taxi and before we knew it we were on our way. My head was spinning. I hadn't prepared myself for any of this.

Matt reached across and gently touched my chin, causing my head to turn and face him. "I've missed you, sweetheart."

"Please don't say that, Matt. You know how much you've hurt me, and I'm just turning the corner and getting on with my life."

Matt paid the driver and led me up to our old front door. The house smelt familiar; comforting. It smelt of Matt. The Matt that I had adored. He took my coat and I felt myself start to crumble.

"Jude, I don't know where it all went wrong."

"I think perhaps it all went wrong when you slept with Deb. Jog any memories for you? Because believe me, they haunt me every day. So if *you've* forgotten, then please allow me to remind you."

"Jude, you say it as if we planned to hurt you. Your sister means nothing to me. She never has done. It's just we were both there feeling miserable and neglected. We needed to feel loved. I missed your loving, baby. It was *you* I wanted, not her. It's always been you."

"Look, Matt, I *do* understand that I left you over here on your own, and for that I'm truly sorry, but…"

"So you can see that we were both responsible then?"

"Well, I can see that…"

Matt placed his fingers over my lips. "Shhhhhhhhhhh. Let's not go there now."

He touched the side of my face tenderly and ran his fingers through my hair. "God, I've missed you. You're still my beautiful girl you know."

The familiarity of his sensual touch melted me to mush. I'd longed for this moment for months. Not only had I fantasised about it, I'd physically ached for it. And now it was here. It was happening. Me and Matt, together again, in one another's arms.

Our lips met, tenderly at first, but before I knew it, we were ripping each other's clothes off and were reunited in the flesh once more like reckless animals; against the wall and then onto the bed. It felt good. It felt comfortable. I felt alive.

"Like a glove," he whispered, smiling as he entered me skin to skin. We both knew what the other liked, and the pleasure was immense. It was as if we'd channelled all of our pain into our lovemaking and, my God, it was good. When it was over, I pleaded for more, and we carried on pleasuring each other until we eventually fell asleep, our bodies hot and clammy with exhaustion. The only words we'd spoken since our initial conversation were those of pure lust and desire.

Chapter Twenty-Two

I awoke to find Matt still sleeping next to me. The events from the previous night raced quickly through my mind. Feeling shocked and ashamed at what had happened, I gathered up my clothes, slipped them on quietly by the front door, crept out and called a cab back to my rented room.

Hands shaking, I placed my keys down on the side table, and immediately spotted the card I'd picked when I first arrived. 'CONSEQUENCES – make wise loving choices' was staring me in the face.

Pacing around the floor, with no clue what to do, I felt utterly dreadful. That all-too-familiar feeling of being out of control had returned with a vengeance. What would Annie say if she was with me? Her voice suddenly popped into my head. "Return to the steps, darlings, every day."

I took a deep breath and sat down on the floor with the twelve steps written in front of me. One by one I absorbed them, relating them to my current situation, admitting I was powerless, asking for help, admitting my shortcomings, and praying only for what Pure Love wanted for me.

After about an hour of solid focus, I felt clear and calm enough to get up and make some tea. As I walked over to the kitchenette, I realised there were seven missed calls from Matt on my phone which I'd put on silent for last night's meal.

I took a deep breath and thought about how best to handle this situation. What would Pure Love want me to do? Two images flashed vividly through my mind. The first was the Devil card that had come up in my reading with Rose. I realised that last night, I had danced to the Devil's tune once again. Only *this* time I could see that I also had the power to set myself free if I wanted to. The second image was of Guy's kind face. The man who had supported me, encouraged me, walked me to the bus stop, driven me to meditation classes, and yet asked for nothing in return.

For the first time since the day I met him, I didn't crave Matt. I didn't want his touch, his words, his intensity. I wanted to be free. I wanted to recover, to be strong, to be successful, to be happy. And if last night was what was needed to make me see this clearly, then I thanked Pure Love for the opportunity.

I took my phone off silent, and made myself a cuppa before jumping in the shower to cleanse myself of Matt. As I stood there under the hot water, I imagined any power he once had over me, running down the drain. I scrubbed my teeth and tongue vigorously, and spat the taste of him down the sink.

As I dried myself, the phone rang. It was Matt again. I ignored the call and continued to get myself ready, determined not to jump to his demands.

Once I'd dressed myself and dried my hair, I decided to call him.

"Oh, Jude, I've been going out of my mind. Where did you go? How do you think I felt when I woke up and saw that you were gone?"

"Matt, we didn't do much talking last night, but there's stuff that needs to be said."

"Ok, I'm listening."

"Last night was about closure for me. I thought I still loved you and wanted you, but when I woke up this morning, I realised that wasn't the case. It felt wrong."

"Wrong? How can you say it felt wrong? You were begging for more for Christ's sake. Jude, it's you and me. We fit together. We'll never find that again with anyone else; we both know that."

"It's not enough for me, Matt – not anymore."

"What, so you're going to leave me here on my own again then? Like you did before? Can't you see how much that hurt me, Jude, and yet here you are, about to repeat history."

"I'm sorry if you see it that way, Matt."

"Let me come over, Jude. Where are you staying? Let's talk this through properly. Come on, babe. Let's start afresh. Let me show you how I feel. Let's get you pregnant, like we planned. You *do* want a baby don't you?"

"It's too late, Matt. My life's moved on. And no, I don't want a baby at this moment in time. I have plans. Exciting plans."

"But what about the turtle doves you painted me? Mated for life, eh? Well, I guess that was all a load of bollocks then."

"I meant it at the time, Matt. I really did, with all my heart. But then my heart got broken, and now I'm fixing it."

"So what's his name then?"

"There's no one else, Matt. Just me and a handful of wonderful friends. They're all I need right now."

"What, so that's it then?"

"I guess it is, yes. I'll get the ball rolling when I get back home and we can get the divorce underway."

"Oh right, so I suppose you'll be stinging me for all I've got then?"

"Actually, Matt, I don't want anything from you. I have all I need. I wish you all the best. Goodbye, Matt." I hung up the phone.

I'd done it. I'd broken free. And it felt wonderful.

A few minutes later, there was a knock on the door. I answered it tentatively to find Meeta standing there looking dreadful.

"Jude, I am so sorry for what happened last night. I did not know Prakash had told Matt you were here. I am so angry with him."

"Please don't be angry with him, Meeta. It's not Prakash's fault. I'm the one who should be sorry. I put you in a difficult position."

"Are you ok, Jude? I have been so worried."

"I'm absolutely fine. Now come on in and let me make you a peppermint tea."

"Did you sort things out with Matt?"

I thought for a moment and then smiled. "Do you know what, Meeta, my friend? Yes, we did."

"You still go home tonight?"

"Yes. So let's do something fabulous today."

"What do you like to do?"

"Well…what I'd really like to do is go to a kundalini yoga class with you, and to do some cooking with Gulab. Just like old times."

We hugged each other tightly, and so began a magical day of fun, friendship and sisterhood. And as the darkness drew in, we bid our farewells, and I headed home with a large case full of goodies, and a freshly baked Chai Masala cake in my bag.

As I waited at the airport, I mulled over my visit to India and was thankful for everything that had happened. I couldn't wait to see Saffie, and show her what I'd bought, and I looked forward to Wednesday evening's meeting; to tell Annie and the group all about my hiccup with Matt, and how the twelve steps had led me to closure.

I realised that in just a few months, my life had transformed from a place of darkness and deep despair, to one of hope and positivity. And for the first time in ages, I felt glad to be me.

But the person I had thought about most during my time away, was Guy. I didn't really know what I wanted from him; I just knew I wanted him in my life. Without too much thought, I messaged him.

'Hi Guy, it's Jude. I hope you're ok? Have had an enlightening time in Punjab. Would love to tell you about it. Flight's due in at eight-thirty tonight. Don't suppose you fancy giving me a lift home? Will gladly reimburse your petrol J. No worries if you're busy. Hope to see you soon. J x'

I boarded the plane, not knowing whether I'd be taken home by bus or by Guy. Either way, it didn't matter, I thought. I was happy to be going home to start my new adventures.

I took out my notepad and pen, and starting listing the items I'd bought for the shop, along with the cost prices while they were still fresh in my mind. On a separate sheet, I made a note of what I thought the items would sell for, and was keen to know what Saffie would think too. It would be interesting to see if we were thinking along the same lines, as this had always been Saff's territory up until now.

"Beautiful scarf and brooch," commented the air hostess as she leant over to pass me my meal. "Where did you get them from? My sister would love something like that for Christmas."

"Funnily enough, I bought them at a bazaar in Patiala. I've got loads in my case to take back home. I'll be selling them in my gift shop."

"Ooh, really? Well, if I give you my address, will you post me one of each? Those colours would be perfect on her."

"I can, with pleasure, but what about the Christmas post? We've probably missed the guaranteed time by now. I tell you what, would you like the ones I'm wearing? They're literally fresh on for the flight."

"Why not? That sounds great. Thank you. Let me finish dishing these dinners out and I'll be back with some money."

I removed the emerald silk scarf and jewelled brooch immediately for fear of spilling plane food down them, and popped them carefully into a brown paper bag I'd got at the airport. If that wasn't confirmation that these items would sell well, then I didn't know what would be. The hostess didn't even discuss price, she just wanted them. I couldn't wait to tell Saffie.

The rest of the flight passed quickly. I finished reading the inspiring book that Annie had leant me, and then dozed until we touched down.

My huge case was waiting for me on the revolving belt, and I asked the man standing next to me if he'd mind helping me wrestle it to the ground and onto my trolley, which he kindly did. I turned my phone back on to find no messages, so I headed for the bus station.

But as I emerged from the airport building and went to join the queue, a message came through and I realised I'd only just got a signal.

On my way, Jude. Will meet you in Car Park C. Guy J

I headed towards Car Park C to find Guy already there waiting with his usual friendly smile.

"Hey, how was your trip?" He lifted my case into the boot. "Blimey! What's in here, a collection of boulders? You trying to give me a hernia or something?" He winked.

"New stock for The Treasure Chest, Guy. And I'm very excited about it. Thanks so much for picking me up."

"Ah, no worries. I was only sitting at home with Phoebe anyway. So? Tell me all about it, I'm intrigued."

"Well, the reason I went back was to catch up with a couple of special ladies who had been so kind to me when I went to live out there. We had some really lovely times together. And I also took the opportunity to buy some stock for the shop, and order some meditation bits for Grace."

"Sounds cool. So, did you hook up with your husband? Ex-husband, whatever he is?"

"Well I didn't intend to, but yes, we hooked up."

Guy turned his head to look the other way. "And how did it go?"

"It was a bit of a rollercoaster to be honest with you, and it caused me to wobble big-time. But thanks to the twelve steps, and thanks to Annie and you guys, I was able to recognise that I had the power to get off whenever I wanted. I just had to ask for the courage and strength."

"So, do you still love him? I mean, do you want to sort things out?"

"Do you know, Guy, I thought I *did* still love him. Even after what he'd done. I loved him so much that I believed there could never be anyone else. That no one else could ever come close to what we had. I'd kind of accepted that I was destined for a lonely future."

"And now?"

"Now I realise that what we had was unhealthy. It wasn't real; it was too dreamlike. It couldn't last, and it certainly didn't survive the challenging times. But I needed to spend time with him again to really see that."

"Hence your message about the enlightening time over there?"

"Exactly. But if it wasn't for the steps, and for friends like Annie, Saffie and you, I'd be back there in his arms again, believing his every word, and waiting on him hand and foot. So, thank you."

Guy looked at me and smiled. "All part of the service, madame."

He pulled into my car parking space outside my flat. It was cold and dark, and a frost had already started to form on the cars.

"Fancy a cuppa? I've got the most amazing cake in my bag, freshly baked by my wonderful friend, Gulab. Chai Masala. Can I tempt you with a slice?"

Guy looked at his watch. "Hmmm. Ten o'clock. It's past my bedtime you know. Oh, go on then, I'll make an exception and have a quick cuppa, as it's you." He opened the boot. "I suppose you want me to break my back, carrying this beast up for you as well then, do you? I tell you what, this cake had better be nice."

Chapter Twenty-Three

It was Tuesday morning and I didn't want to wake up. As I peeled my eyelids back to the open position, I wished I'd taken an extra day off to recover from a hectic past few days. But once I'd got myself into the upright position, I remembered how I couldn't wait to see Saffie and show her all the wonderful things I'd bought for The Treasure Chest...

The bus ride in was a bit of a struggle with my huge heavy case in tow, but fortunately there were enough kind people around who were willing to help. Reaching my destination, and ignoring a fundraising rotary-club elf, who was shaking a money box in my face, I lugged it over the threshold of the shop with a huge sigh of relief.

"Aha! The wanderer returns!"

"As if I wouldn't. Give us a hug."

"So, how was it? And what the heckidy heck have you got in *there*?"

"Saff, you wouldn't believe it. The trip was a real rollercoaster of highs and lows."

"Uh oh, don't tell me...Matt was involved."

"Yes, he was, Saff, but I didn't go looking for him, he walked in on a meal I was at. Anyway, long story short, I went back with him, we slept together..."

"Oh, Jude, no!"

"Yes, Saff, it happened, but it took for me to do that to realise that I don't want him anymore. It's over, and I'm going to file for divorce."

"Yay! That's brilliant news, honey. Good riddance to bad rubbish. He was never good enough for my lovely Jude." She hugged me again.

"But the rest of the trip was fab. It was great to spend time with my friends. Meeta's pregnant, so that was a wonderful surprise. And we did some serious haggling in the bazaars. I can't wait to show you what's in my case. Oh, and the money came through from Dad's house too."

"Crikey, it *has* been a busy few days! Let's stick the kettle on then and have a look in this case. I'm intrigued!" I wheeled the case through to our empty Box of Delights. "So what time did you get home last night?"

"I got in about ten-ish. Guy dropped me home, bless him."

"Oh, did he now?" Saff winked as she handed me my coffee.

"Yes, he did. Now try some of this wonderful cake, made by the not-so-fair hands of my lovely friend, Gulab."

"Ooh, don't mind if I do. Smells delicious. Anyway, Judith, we have digressed. What's going on with you and Guy? Is it luuur-rrrrvvvv? He *is* rather cute."

"To be honest with you, Saff, I don't know what it is. I do really like him and I thought about him a lot while I was away, but then again, I thought about you lots too."

"Oh my God, you're not after a threesome are you?!" Saffie giggled.

"And I thought about Annie too."

"Hey, this is turning into a full-blown orgy! That'd be enough to finish poor old Annie off!" Unable to ignore her silliness any longer, we both had a good old chuckle, slurped our coffees and finished our cake. "Well, that was delish. Now show me, show me."

I began to remove and lay out the silk scarves and wall hangings, pashminas, brooches, bangles, beaded slippers and bags, and explained what I'd paid for them all. Saffie was thrilled to bits and we spent much of the day deciding on prices, setting things out, and displaying samples in the window.

Towards the end of the day, I received a message from Annie, asking how I was, so I decided to call in on her on my way home, to catch up and return her book.

As always, she greeted me with a warm sunny smile, and I

was delighted to see her looking stronger on her feet. I told her all about my eventful few days in Patiala and my awakening. Annie listened and nodded along with interest, and she seemed pleased that I'd overcome another big hurdle.

"So, darling, a little birdie tells me that you asked Guy to pick you up and drive you home last night."

"Yes I did. It feels wonderful having such a dependable friend in my life; one who understands me."

"And is that *all* he is to you, darling, a friend?"

I felt myself blush. "Well to tell you the truth, Annie, I really like him. I mean, I reeeaally like him. I thought about him a lot while I was away. But the thing is, I don't know if he wants anything more than friendship. He hasn't tried to kiss me – well, only a peck on the cheek last night when he left my flat. And I don't feel the way I felt with Matt when I'm with him. So how do I know whether I'm just trying to fill another void?"

"Well, darling, do you feel that you want him, or do you feel that you need him?"

"I guess it's more of a want rather than a need. With Matt it was a need. A desperate need."

"It was co-dependency then, darling, but you're stronger now."

"Yes, and I can see that now. But the last thing I want to do is spoil a friendship with Guy, so maybe I should just be grateful for what we already have."

"Yes, you must be grateful, Jude, because it's precious. And so is Guy. And if it's meant to develop, then it will happen, darling, it will."

"You're right, as always, Annie."

"It comes with being old, darling," she winked, "but I feel I need to tell you that Guy seems to be sharing the same sentiments and concerns as you at the moment. He really likes you too. Reeeaally likes you! But he doesn't want to take advantage of you while you're healing, or get in the way of your recovery. He's a sensitive soul that one."

"Oh, I see. And what do you think? Do you think we're both ready?"

Annie closed her eyes for a moment. "I don't suppose you have your cards with you do you, darling?"

I rummaged around in my huge bag which I hadn't yet unpacked from India. "Yes I do…right here."

"Good, because I feel we need to pick one and ask for some guidance. Pass them over, darling."

Annie shuffled the deck with her large hands, fanned the cards out, chose one and turned it over in front of us. 'SPIRITUAL UNION – joyous bliss'.

We looked at each other and laughed. "Well, if that's not confirmation, darling, then I don't know what is."

I felt my heart begin to swell. I was in no great rush to be completely intense with someone again; not with the shop about to reopen, but the thought of having love, understanding, companionship and someone handsome to cuddle up to *did* sound highly appealing.

"Leave it with me, darling. I'll see you right."

Chapter Twenty-Four

The Box of Delights was coming on a treat. Furnished with whites and brights, it looked very angelic. Our weekly activities had fallen into place nicely and I was able to get cracking with the advertising and give the finer details to Guy to produce some leaflets.

Monday evenings would offer an hour of kundalini yoga, followed by an hour of meditation with Grace. We'd play it by ear and see what the demand was. Shona was offering her acupuncture services on a Tuesday, Toni would be in the shop on Wednesdays doing spiritual healing, Rose would be giving readings on Thursdays, and Grace was back in on Fridays, offering massage.

We didn't know how it would fair, but we both had a good feeling about it. The ladies would pay us a percentage of their takings, so it was in our interest as well as theirs to push the services. Luckily, there wasn't much in the way of competition in the high street, and many of our regular customers were loyal and fairly spiritual too. So this was where we would focus initially, handing out flyers with every purchase, and tempting them with introductory deals, in the hope that they would tell their friends.

With Christmas only a week away, the shop was busy; especially so as we offered a free festive gift-wrapping service at this time of year which always proved popular. When it came to wrapping pressies, Saffie and I were the masters and could even multitask too. The phone rang and I popped it under my chin, allowing me to continue with the tape, the ribbons and the bows.

"Jude, it's Guy. How you doing?"

"Oh, hi. Er, I'm busy…but great thanks. You ok?"

"Fine and dandy, ta. Listen, I won't keep you. Just to say that I received the copy for your flyers which all looks fine, so I'll get onto that now. Oh…and…I wondered if you fancied seeing a film on Friday? Anyway, no need to answer now. Hopefully I'll have these done for you today so I'll call in with them later. The sooner you can start handing these out the better."

"Cinema sounds great. And thanks for sorting the flyers. You're an angel. Well, you know, a masculine one, not a pink and fluffy one."

Guy chuckled. "Cool. See you later then, and don't work too hard!"

"I'd say the same, Guy, but I want my flyers! Only teasing. Take care and see you later."

I put the phone down, bagged up the lady's gifts, and sorted her change from the till, feeling very conscious that Saffie was staring over for my attention.

"Cinema, eh? I take it that's a 'date' then?" She gave the back of my neck a little tickle.

"Oh, I don't know, Saff. I'm kind of hoping it is, but I don't want to spoil things. We get on so well…you know…as friends."

"Well, my lovely…when you don't know what to do…best have a brew," and off Saffie went to the kitchen to make us a coffee, singing "Love is in the air…everywhere I look around…" and giggling to herself.

As promised, Guy popped in later with the flyers, hot off the press. They had just the right vibe about them, making me realise even more how tuned in he was to our vision.

"Got your meeting tonight, Jude? I hear Annie's feeling strong enough to get there if she can."

"Yes, great news isn't it? I've missed the group, you know. They're a funny bunch really, but we've all grown rather fond of each other."

"That happens, Jude. It's all about accepting people for who they are. I guess we're all a bit odd when you think about it; all got our funny little ways."

"Makes life interesting I suppose."

"Are you up for meditation tomorrow night?"

"Ooh yes, most definitely. Anything to keep me sane!"

"Great. I'll pick you up normal time then?"

"That would be lovely. Thanks, Guy. You *are* good to me."

"And you're sure you're up for Friday too? Don't want to overload you with my good looks, wit and charm. It's just Phoebe's turned me down, and I can't go on my own now can I?" He winked.

"Sounds like a perfect end to a fabulous week."

"Cool. Well, enjoy your group tonight."

"You too, Guy."

"And I'll see you tomorrow." He strolled casually out of the shop and gave me a little wave through the window as he disappeared home.

* * *

The meeting was really productive and it was great to have Annie back with us. She *did* look a tad frail still, but she hid it well and refused to give in. We focused on the 'one day at a time/just for today' concept which was incredibly helpful for everyone to take on board. It means that whenever we get overwhelmed by life's happenings, we need only focus on today; not tomorrow or next week, and not on the ifs, buts and maybes. This enables us to step out of our fears and into our power of the here and now.

Annie paired us up and asked if we'd share our experiences of this idea with each other over the Christmas period. We wouldn't be meeting for a couple of weeks, but this way, we had Annie as a contact, and also our partner to help keep us on track. I was paired with the lovely Ray, who found this concept tremendously helpful, given his current debt problems.

Our Thursday-night meditation session with Grace covered a similar theme; focusing on the present moment to keep us sane over the Christmas period. So many people were run ragged;

hosting large numbers and trying to please everyone with their cooking skills and their gift choices. I for one was delighted to have broken free from all these expectations, and looked forward to pulling a cracker with Saffie and Sol, tucking into a roast together, slouching in our pyjamas, and nodding off in front of the telly whenever we wanted to. And I was mightily thankful that I wouldn't be missing Matt over the festive period too…wishing he'd call, craving his cuddles or feeling like half a person without him.

I'd give Mum a call on Christmas morning and wish her and Francine a lovely day, but that was as far as family went now, and I was absolutely fine with that.

Before I knew it, Friday was here, and wanting to make an effort for my evening with Guy, I took time to apply body scrubs and creams, ensuring that I was smooth all over and smelling divine. Nurturing my body made me feel sensual, and this was an important part of who I wanted to be. I'd thought carefully about what underwear to put on, and decided to go for a pale-pink laced camisole which ruched up at the centre to reveal my midriff, and a small pair of matching lace knickers. The camisole flattered and framed my breasts, making me look womanly, without looking tarty, and the knickers left more to the imagi-nation than a thong, but had a subtle sheerness to them. I hoped Guy would appreciate my choice, as I didn't have a clue what he liked in that department.

I scrunch-dried my hair into natural waves and loosely braided the front section from one side to the other, giving the impression of a headband, which looked really pretty. I decided to play it down on the clothing front – casual but feminine, opting for black leggings and knee-high boots, a long, oyster-pink fluffy jumper which fell off the shoulder, my favourite moonstone pendant, an across-the-body beaded bag, and an array of skinny bangles.

I spent time on my eye makeup, creating smoky grey lids

with feline black liner, and finishing the look with a sheer pearlescent lip gloss, perfect for kissing. Feeling totally gorgeous and rather excited, I changed the bedding and spritzed the room with a warm and sensuous amber musk, feeling totally ready to commit to new beginnings.

When I saw him pull into the car park, I made my way downstairs and jumped into the passenger seat.

"Ooh, you smell nice, Jude. Even better than my car freshener!" He winked. "How was your day?"

"Hectic! Still, shouldn't grumble. How was yours?"

"Mine was busy too, tying everything up for the Christmas break. I'm off now until the new year. So pleased to finally have some time out."

"Ooh, lucky you. Mind you, I finish tomorrow and have a few days' rest to look forward to."

"Cool. What you doing for Christmas?"

"Going to Saffie's. We have our day planned out nicely. I'll turn up in my pyjamas late morning for a sherry while we get the dinner on the go, then we'll spend some time with Sol, then stuff our faces with calories galore, before falling asleep on the sofa with a wine or two. I'll crash round there and spend Boxing Day recovering. How about you?"

"Ooh, well, mine will be a tad more sober than yours. In fact, I'm just gonna order myself a monster curry and vegetate on the sofa with Phoebe."

"What, you're spending it alone?"

"Yeah; it's through choice though, Jude, so no violins please. I *did* get an invite round me mum's, but my sisters will be over there and I can't be doing with all their dramas. Don't get me wrong, I do care about them, but they demand an awful lot of attention, and I'm kind of done with all that if you get what I mean."

"Totally. Sometimes it's healthier to love people from a distance."

"You're absolutely right there, Jude. If people don't want to help themselves, it's detrimental to your own recovery to get too involved. I like to picture a bridge in my mind, and see myself crossing to a place of recovery, then telling the person I care about to join me when they're ready to do the same."

"That's a good one. Only sometimes it's probably best if they don't ever join you!"

"Are you referring to your ex by any chance?"

"However did you guess?! Anyway, enough about him. What we going to see tonight?"

"*Life of Pi*. Hope that's ok. Have you read the book?"

"Can't say I have."

"Well you must. It's wonderful. And I'm hoping the film will do it justice."

Guy bought us a huge milkshake each and a tub of popcorn to share, and we both got totally absorbed in the film. He was right, the story was amazing and incredibly thought-provoking, and all the way home, we debated over which version of the story we each believed to be true.

"Well, here you go, madame," announced Guy as we reached the flats. "Can I walk you to your door?"

With butterflies in my tummy, I replied, "That would be very kind. What a gentleman you are."

He gave me his elbow and I linked my arm through his as we ascended the stairs.

"Care for a coffee?" I asked as I turned the key in the door.

"Ah, thanks for the offer, Jude, but you have work tomorrow. Get yourself some sleep and maybe we'll catch up over Christmas, eh?!"

"Oh, ok then. Errr…yes…let's do that then."

Although Guy's words were kind, I couldn't help but feel rejected, disappointed and deflated, particularly as I'd gone to incredible lengths to look my best from every angle, and to smell positively delicious. And as we waved goodbye to each other, I felt utterly confused as to what our relationship actually was.

Unable to get to sleep, I tried applying some logic to the situation. Without a shadow of a doubt we were friends, and good ones at that. And Guy obviously cared about me and enjoyed my company or he wouldn't have invited me out. But maybe that was as far as he wanted it to go for now. After all, an interested male would surely jump at the chance of a welcome invitation at the end of an evening date. No, I didn't get it, and I hardly got a wink of sleep, trying to figure it out.

I picked a card for guidance as soon as I got up. It said 'CONFIDENCE – be bold and take charge' and showed a picture of a fearless cougar. But my head was so muddled that I didn't really have a clue about how that related to me. With a heavy heart, I trundled off to the shop, hoping I would find the energy to function effectively today.

"Blimey, you look tired! Been up all night have you, Judith?"

Saffie's teasing was always well-meant, and had things gone to plan, I would probably have giggled and blushed profusely. But instead, I felt like crying, and I hated feeling this vulnerable again. I shook my head, letting her know that all was not great.

"I can't make head nor tail of it all, Saff. We get on so well. Conversation is interesting but easy at the same time. We share the same sense of humour and the same spiritual interests. He invites me out, picks me up, treats me like a lady, walks me home like a true gent, and then nothing advances further than a quick peck on the cheek. I guess he just wants to be friends."

"Like hell he does! Jude, he's not blind. Bloody hell, look at you; you're totally gorgeous on the inside and out. What man in their right mind wouldn't want a slim, beautiful, compassionate young woman with a mane of long golden locks on his arm?" She scratched her head. "Right, there's one of two reasons why not. Either he's gay, or he's not being completely straight with you. Haha! Get it? He's either gay or not straight!!!"

I managed a semi smile at Saffie's daftness. "Well I'm pretty sure he's not gay."

"So then, talk to him. Find out what's going on. He likes you, Jude – anyone could tell that a mile off."

"Well, Annie said that too. Only she hinted that he might be worried about setting me back."

"Well, even more reason to talk to him then. Be honest, Jude. Tell him you feel confused."

"Yeah, I guess you're right. Maybe he thinks friendship is easier to handle. You know, keeping things simple."

"Haha! My sentiments exactly! Life is definitely simpler being single. But that doesn't mean it's right for everyone. And I think that you and Guy would make the perfect match. Honestly, you'd make the most beautiful babies."

I laughed. "So what do you think I should do then?"

"Call him. Invite him over, or ask if you could call in at his place. Take a deep breath and just go for it."

A steady flow of last-minute Christmas shoppers put our conversation on hold, but deep down I knew that I couldn't ignore the sentiments of my best friend and my cards. I was sure they were right. It was time to be bold and to take charge.

Chapter Twenty-Five

The previous evening, I had referred to and worked through the twelve steps, praying only for what Pure Love wanted for me, and the will to carry it out. I knew I had to speak with Guy and clarify things, but I also knew that I would just have to accept his reply, whatever that would be.

I had also called Raymondo and we'd chatted about what was going on for us both. Discussing the other's issues, and relating them to the 'just for today' concept, really helped to put things into perspective. Emotions always seemed to be heightened at this time of year. I guess it was the expectation to have the perfect Christmas. My definition of a perfect Christmas would be to know where I stood with Guy, and then to enjoy a fun and relaxing day with Saffie. But today was Christmas Eve, so time was of the essence.

I messaged Guy, asking if we could meet for a chat. Either I could go to him, or he could come to me. Other than wrapping a few gifts for tomorrow, my day was free, and it was good to not have any time constraints for a change. My tummy turned summersaults in anticipation of his reply, but rather than getting completely stressed out, I took deep breaths and allowed these feelings to be my guide.

I kept asking Pure Love to be with me and to work through me to resolve any upsets and restore me to harmony, and I only had to wait a few minutes before Guy messaged me back.

'Hi, Jude. Of course we can have a chat. Probably easier if I come to you. Be there in an hour if that's ok. See you then. G'

I felt relieved at the prospect of getting things sorted, and a little nervous about what I would say, but something told me that whatever happened, things would be ok. I tidied the flat and wrapped up the black onyx key ring I'd bought for Guy, popping it into a cute little silver box with a tiny black bow. It was an inexpensive but meaningful gesture and I hoped he'd like it.

I opened the door to find him looking a little more serious than usual. His eyes weren't quite so twinkly, but he still managed a little joke.

"You called…?"

"Thanks for coming over, Guy. Come in. Let's have a cuppa and a chat."

"Everything ok, Jude?"

"Everything's fine. It's just, I'm feeling a little…well… confused."

"Well we can't have that now, can we? What's up?"

"Well…oh hell, I'm just going to come out and say it. I'm confused about you and me. We seem to get on so well, and I'm very comfortable with you, and I think you're comfortable with me too, and we're spending lots of time together, and we're both single, and you asked me out to the cinema, and I thought…."

"You thought things might progress and they haven't?"

"Well…yes. It's just that things seemed to be going so well on Friday evening. I'd kind of assumed it was a date. But then I invited you in and…"

"And I declined and you felt rejected."

"Errr…yes. And I feel like I just need to know what we are to each other. If you want to keep it as friendship then that's ok; I can accept that. It just feels…"

"Like we should be more than friends?"

"Exactly."

"Well I guess I haven't been very fair to you by not explaining myself clearly then have I? And for that, I'm truly sorry. And I'm glad you've prompted this conversation because you know what us blokes are like. If there's a problem, we disappear into our caves until we have a clear solution."

"And do you have a clear solution?"

"No, but I do have an explanation."

"Ok. Well then, I'd really like to hear it. I mean, to understand how you feel."

I passed him his coffee and we both sat down.

"Right. Well first of all, Jude, I really like you. I think you're beautiful and kind and smart and funny. In fact, you're pretty much my definition of a perfect woman."

"Ok?" I felt myself blush, wondering what was coming next.

"And I'd really like to more than friends. I mean, I'd *really* like that. More than anything."

"But?"

"But, I'm frightened of sabotaging things; of ruining what we have; of hurting you."

"Ok. Well, how do you mean?"

"Look, you know I'm very open about my past. When I'm drunk, I'm a complete and utter bastard. And I have to keep my focus on not slipping back there – you know, to be the person I want to be."

"And that person is very kind and considerate and charming."

"Well, thank you, that's what I'd like to think, but I haven't always been this person."

"And I understand that, Guy. And that's ok with me."

"But it's not ok if I hurt you. You're just too special. And as I explained to you at the meeting, I've hurt a lot of women. I've treated women like shit."

"But that's in the past."

"Yes, but I need you to know what I'm like at my worst, Jude. I didn't just go missing when I was drunk, I was out looking for prostitutes and sleeping with them. It was my mission. I had no respect for any party involved, least of all me. But now I'm in recovery, I have to pray every day to release the guilt and shame of it. Jude, I never want to treat a lady like that again, or involve anyone in my acts of self-indulgence."

"And so it's easier to be single."

"Yes it is. That way I can't hurt anyone."

"And what if that someone sees you for who you truly are, and they believe you've changed."

"But that's the thing, Jude. That selfish arsehole is still a part of who I am. If I slipped back, I could be that person again tomorrow. I can only be the nice me for today. That's all I can promise you – that today I will be sober and kind, and loving, and focused. But I can't promise any more. And that just doesn't feel good enough for anyone, let alone for someone as amazing as you. I can't offer you a future, Jude. I'm too afraid."

"Well, what if I'm prepared to take that chance? After all, Guy, we both know that today is all there really is. And all we can both do is to be honest about how we're feeling, be that good or bad."

"Yeah, I guess so."

"And I can tell you that, just for today, I'd quite like to kiss you."

Guy's frown quickly transformed into a cheeky smile. "Honestly, woman, what *are* you doing to me?"

His phone rang. "Do you mind if I take this? It's a close friend from the fellowship."

"Be my guest." Feeling a lot lighter from understanding the full picture, I took our mugs to the kitchen and flicked the kettle on again. It was thirsty work all this talking. But I couldn't help overhearing the conversation.

"Hello, mate. You ok? What?!" He sounded shocked. "Oh God, ok. Right. Right. Ok, I'll let them know. Yep. Oh, God. Ok, mate. Take care and call me if I can do anything else to help. Ok then, bye now."

I walked back in the room and noticed that Guy was ashen-faced. "Everything ok?"

"Errr...not really. Jude, it's Annie."

"What about her? What's happened?"

"She had another massive heart attack in the night. Managed to call an ambulance. Got rushed to hospital and they operated."

"Well, how's she doing? Can we visit her?"

"Jude, she didn't make it. They couldn't save her. Annie's

dead."

"What? She can't be. Not Annie. Noooooooo." Guy stood up and held me as we sobbed our hearts out into each other.

"Apparently, just before she went, she said that her work here was done."

"But however will we manage without her? She's such a force."

Guy brushed my hair back off my face. "And she still is, Jude. That force will never leave us. Annie's passed that wisdom on. It was her gift; her legacy. And that knowledge can never die so long as we live by it and keep passing it on to others."

He kissed my forehead tenderly. "She's asked that I let everyone know about the funeral. She wanted us all there. She gave a clear verbal list of instructions to the paramedic. I guess she knew her time was up."

"I wouldn't miss it for the world. I'm sure everyone will want to be there too. When is it?"

"Possibly the eighth of January, but it won't be confirmed until after Christmas. The whole world shuts down now doesn't it? No one's allowed to die at Christmas." He let out a big sigh. "She asked if I'd give a reading. God, I wouldn't know where to start."

"You'll be fine, Guy. Perfect in fact. Give yourself some time and the words will come, I'm sure. Now let's have some sweet tea. They say it's good for shock."

As I made our drinks, we shared our memories of Annie. Guy had known her much longer than I had, but that seemed irrelevant somehow. She'd had a massive impact on both of our lives, and without a shadow of a doubt, had aided our recoveries.

"I always said she was an Earth Angel," I smiled. "Only now she's a heavenly one I guess."

Guy agreed. I grabbed the silver box from the worktop. "Here. I got this for you. It's only a little something. Merry Christmas."

Guy looked touched. "For me? Oh, thanks. That's really sweet of you. Can I open it?"

"Yes, why not? It's nearly Christmas after all."

"It's beautiful, Jude. Thank you. I'll pop my keys straight onto it and keep it in my pocket forever. Black onyx, eh? Aren't crystals supposed to have their own meanings? Any idea what black onyx is supposed to do?"

"Not off the top of my head, no. But my trusty book of crystals will tell us I'm sure. Bear with me a mo."

I pulled the book down from my shelf and flicked through until I reached the page for onyx. "Onyx is strength-giving. It provides support in difficult or confusing circumstances and during times of enormous mental or physical stress, centring your energy and aligning it with a higher power."

"Crikey! That sounds pretty darn spot on!"

"Doesn't it just!" I closed the book and looked up at him. "It'll be ok you know, Guy."

"Yeah, I know it will. Thanks for my gift. It's perfect. And so are you." He bent down and kissed me tenderly on the lips.

I suddenly had a flashback. "Annie will see us right. She promised me. That was the last thing she said to me."

We laughed at the irony, enjoyed a hug, and drank our tea. "Tell you what. How about we spend Boxing Day evening together? You know, a proper date. I'll cook. Make up for being such a muppet."

"Sounds great. I've always had a soft spot for muppets by the way. But, hey, what about Phoebe?"

"Well I guess Miss Phoebe will have to get used to the idea of having you around, won't she? Merry Christmas, beautiful Jude."

* * *

Ever the gent, Guy had left me to get on with my last-minute preparations. We were both pretty exhausted from all the emotions, but I felt so relieved we'd been able to talk things through so honestly, and it felt significant that we'd been together when the sad news about Annie came through.

After the rollercoaster that was Christmas Eve, I had slept like a log, and awoke feeling calm, rested, and ready for the festive day ahead with Saffie and Sol.

I always looked forward to a nice long soak in the bath on Christmas morning. It was a bit of a personal tradition. I crumbled my favourite fragranced bubble bar under the running water and immersed myself in the luxurious foam. It felt so good not to be rushing, but nevertheless, I still had to pack my overnight things and an outfit to wear to Guy's tomorrow. I wasn't sure that pyjamas would be wholly appropriate for a first dinner date.

That aside, pyjamas were definitely the order of today, so I rubbed in a scented body balm and put on my favourite snuggie pair, along with some cosy slippers, completing the look with a fluffy dressing gown. The combination of nightwear, daylight and travelling on the bus, however, may have lead to me getting institutionalised, so with that in mind, I decided to push the boat out and get a cab. Saffie was only in the next village after all.

Sol's cheeky little smiling face greeted me at the door. He was nine and just on that border of not being one hundred percent sure if Santa existed, but really wanting it to be true, so going along with the whole thing anyway. I certainly wasn't going to be the one to confirm his fears, and I thoroughly enjoyed playing along with the whole magical concept of flying reindeers and elves.

"Merry Christmas, sweetheart!" I bent down to kiss him and he gave me the most scrumptious hug. The smell of Christmas trees and roasting turkey filled the house.

"Where's Mum?"

"She'll be down in a minute. She's just drying her hair and putting her posh pyjamas on. I've been waiting for you by the window."

Chapter Twenty-Five

"How lovely. I've been excited too. Now tell me, what did Santa bring?"

He ran over to the tree and held up a big box. "A remote control car!"

"Wowzers! That looks rather special! I'm guessing you must've been pretty darn good this year then?" Sol smiled and shrugged. "So did you leave him a note last night? You know, the big guy?"

"Sure did. And he even wrote back, look."

"How cool is that? Well, that must mean you left him and his reindeers a tasty treat then? Only I'm sure he doesn't write back to everyone."

"Sherry, mince pies and carrots."

"Wow. That's enough to make any guy write a note."

"Fancy a game of Guess Who? It's the new edition. I got it in my stocking."

"Well, quite frankly, I can't think of anything I'd rather do, Sol. But on one condition. You have to let me win."

"Why?"

"Well, coz I'm old, and I'm a sore loser."

Sol giggled, enjoying my teasing. By the time we'd played the best of three with Sol emerging as the Guess Who champion, Saffie entered the room with open arms. "Merry Christmas, honey! It's so good to have you here. Isn't it, Sol? Nice to have Auntie Judith?"

"Really nice," Sol agreed.

"And it's really great to be here, so thank you both." We shared a wonderful pyjama'd embrace and Saffie smelt divine.

"Right then, glass of sherry while we peel the spuds? I opened the bottle for Santa last night." She winked.

"Don't mind if I do."

"May as well start as we mean to go on, eh? Here, let's have a mince pie while we're at it. Sol, darling, can you put the Christmas tunes on please?"

We all did a bit of 'Rocking Around The Christmas Tree' in our slippers, and then Sol went off to play with his new car.

"So? Did you sort things with Guy?"

"Thankfully yes. It turned out to be a rather emotional afternoon. Guy was really honest with me, bless him. He's just frightened of hurting me that's all. He knows his priority must always be about keeping on the straight and narrow, and I guess the responsibility of that weighs heavy on his mind, let alone having someone else to consider."

"Well, you'll just have to make sure you don't distract him tooooo much with your womanly charms then won't you, Jude?" She smirked.

"I think I can support him you know, Saff. You know – properly understand and appreciate his fears."

"Well, he certainly seems like he's up for supporting you. See? There you go. Like I said – a match made in heaven. So, is it official then? Are you and Guy, well, you know."

"I believe we are, Saff, and it feels good. He's offered to cook me dinner tomorrow night. Our first official date."

"Crikey, best not be too hung-over then. Speaking of which, let's have another sherry and raise a glass to you and Guy. Here's to love!"

"To love!"

Saffie seemed so happy for me, and I made a decision not to tell her about Annie's passing as I didn't want her worrying or feeling bad. But as we sat down at the table to tuck in to our delicious feast of a meal, a feeling of complete love and gratitude washed over me and I raised a glass to my angel, my saviour, whose guiding light had shone so brightly, it showed me the way out of the dark.

Chapter Twenty-Six

I looked at the clock. Its bold red response told me unmistakeably that it was six in the morning on Monday the eighth of January. I pulled the duvet over my head and tried to block out all evidence of the day. But it was no use, today was happening whether I liked it or not, and I sure wasn't going to miss Annie's send off. I laid there for a while, rerunning the conversations we'd shared, and all the things she'd said in the short time I'd known her that had meant so much.

Then suddenly, as if she was sitting right next to me, I heard her voice as clear as day:

"Jude, darling, we have to accept that all good things come to an end. And when they end, wonderful new things have room to take their place."

It took me back to the day I visited her in hospital. I hadn't realised the significance of her words on that day, but I sure did now.

In this very moment, and for the first time ever, the cycle of life made perfect sense. I looked out of the window to the barren trees beyond, and I understood that their emptiness would soon be replaced with healthy new life. And whether that life took the form of green leaves or fruit, it would either provide food for wildlife or oxygen and shade for us humans on a hot day. Nothing was wasted and everything mattered. But in order to appreciate it fully, the process of death followed by birth followed by death and so on, had to be accepted as a necessary change; Annie's death included.

At that precise moment, a fluffy white feather floated gently past my line of vision and I somehow knew that this was a comforting message that she was still around.

I made myself some breakfast and tried to decide on what to wear to the funeral. It was cold and drizzly outside, and certainly not the most pleasant conditions for a burial. The dress code had been specified as 'non black : the brighter the better', and so with Annie in mind, I opted for an aqua-coloured knitted dress, a wide red belt and matching bangle, and my oldest but most favourite pair of red leather boots. I would finish it off with my scarlet lipstick and turquoise earrings from India.

"Here's to you, Annie," I said aloud, slurping the last mouthful of coffee and raising my mug to the heavens. "May you rest in peace and continue to shine your loving brightness wherever you go."

I could almost feel Annie's approval as I added each item to my ensemble, as if we were somehow getting ready together and sharing a giggle.

"There! Is that bright enough for you, Annie?" I smiled.

I opened the door to Guy who was bang on time in collecting me. He was wearing a Hawaiian shirt over a long sleeved t-shirt and looked as cheeky as ever, if a little nervous. Not many people were handsome enough to carry off this look, but Guy most definitely was. I couldn't help but hum the theme tune from *Hawaii Five-O* as he walked in.

"Very funny, Jude."

"Sorry, I couldn't resist." I gave him a hug and a kiss, and we squeezed each other tightly. Noticing the transfer of red lipstick from my lips to his, I quickly gave them a wipe. "Maybe not the best look for your reading," I commented, and gave a twirl, amused by the vividness of my outfit. "So? How do *I* look?!"

"Like a Bloody Smurf!"

"Gee thanks!"

"That's the name of a cocktail you know. Blue curacao and grenadine. A Bloody Smurf. Very tasty!" He winked. "A bit like you."

"Well if I'm a Bloody Smurf, then you must be a totally tropical pinã colada. Oh no, wait...a Blue Hawaii!"

"I'll have you know I'm an alcohol free zone thanks very much missy. My body is a temple don't you know. So I guess I'm more of a mocktail than a cocktail these days. Fruity with a bit of fizz"

"Sounds delicious! And no hangover either. I might have to try it sometime."

"Well, you never know…if you play your cards right and all that… Anyway, come on, Smurfette, are you ready?"

"I think so. But wait…hang on a moment. Can you smell something?"

"No? Like what?"

"Oh, I don't know. Like…Hawaiian Tropic?"

He rolled his eyes and shook his head. "Well, aren't you the funny one today then?! Now hurry up or I'm going to have to put you on the naughty step when we get back. And if that doesn't sort you out then we'll have to resort to a good old-fashioned smacked bottom."

"Ok, ok, I'm coming, I'm coming." I grabbed my keys and linked my arm through Guy's. It was good to have a laugh together. We both needed to release some tension, and I felt sure that Annie was enjoying the amusement too.

We arrived at the cemetery in plenty of time, and as we drove slowly along the winding lane, through the gardens and up to the chapel, the sun broke through the clouds.

"Oh, look, Guy, a rainbow. Isn't it beautiful?"

He smiled. "Maybe it's Annie's rainbow-bridge to heaven."

"Ahh, that's a nice thought. I like that. Annie's colourful ascension." I turned my gaze from the rainbow to Guy's face. "How are you feeling?"

"Nervous. But ok. I want to do this for Annie and I feel so honoured to be asked. I just hope I don't muck it up." He pulled up the handbrake and I placed my hand over his.

"You'll be fine. In fact, you'll be amazing. Now come here." I put my arms around him and he hugged me tightly. "She'll be with you, you know."

The car park was filling up fast and it wasn't long before the funeral director appeared, walking humbly up the driveway in front of the hearse. We made our way over to the entrance of the chapel, awaiting the arrival of Annie, and I was delighted to see that every member of our group was there too, along with a sea of faces I didn't recognise.

As her coffin came into view, I was overwhelmed at how many flowers surrounded her. The beautifully arranged words, MUM, SISTER and NAN, made me appreciate that she didn't only play the role of wise leader, confidante, and friend to many, but wore several family hats too. Unable to swallow down the lump in my throat, I felt myself wobble, and the tears began to flow.

Two men lifted the front half of the coffin onto their shoulders, whilst two funeral guys held up the rear. Recognising a likeness, I gathered they must've been Annie's son and grandson, and they walked solemnly but proudly past us, into the chapel, their pathway lit by the now-beaming sun.

As we followed in behind, we were each handed an order-of-service booklet, and told that the seating on the left-hand side was for blood family, and that the right was for her Al-Anon family. And there laid Annie at the front; in pride of place; head of both families, I thought.

The chapel was full to bursting with brightly coloured guests, and a huge feeling of love filled the room. I took my seat next to Guy, and looked down at the cover of the order of service. There, smiling back at me, was my friend Annie. Optimistic, joyful and incredibly knowing. Guy gripped my hand tightly and I flicked through the pages to see when his turn would be. And there it was – his full name printed in black and white before me, listed directly beneath the eulogy: 'Reading by Guy Swann.'

I'd only know Guy for a couple of months, and we'd only been together for a matter of days. Nevertheless, we knew so much about each other, and yet I'd never thought to ask his surname. But suddenly, the final mystery piece of Rose's reading puzzle slotted into place. The image of a swan that she received when I was there, was about Guy. Guy Swann. My new man. This gorgeous gent who had picked me up from Saffie's on Boxing Day and cooked me a heavenly meal with pure goodness in his heart and no expectations in return. This beautiful soul who had been so incredibly honest with me about his heartfelt fears. I knew that Annie would be so pleased we'd worked things out, and who knows, maybe she'd had a hand in our resolution too.

The eulogy, given by her son, was both funny and touching, and I felt privileged to listen to and discover things about Annie the mother, Annie the wife, Annie the sister and Annie the gran.

And then it was Guy's turn to take centre stage, being introduced as Annie's 'right-hand man when it came to recovery', which everybody smiled at. Clearly and calmly, he began to speak.

"Like many of us in this room today, I owe so much to Annie. And like many of us in this room today, Annie spent many years struggling away in a dark lonely place, feeling scared and confused. But then, when she'd had enough of struggling, she discovered a group of understanding people who were willing to share their experiences with her, and together they took great comfort in following a twelve-step programme which could lead them back to sanity. She gradually learnt to let go of her deep sorrow, despair and anger with the world, and when she did, she made room instead for peace, joy and acceptance. This was no bearing of what went on around her. It was her own inward journey.

"Then once she was strong enough, she reached out her hand and offered help to whoever was ready to take it. And although I'm sorry that Annie had to struggle, I am also very grateful that she did. Because it made her compassionate towards other people like me, and as a result, her loving wisdom touched many of us sitting before me. That's why we're here. Because we love her, and we want to show her our gratitude, but also because she suffered.

"I feel so lucky that our paths crossed when they did, and incredibly honoured to be standing here right now. As always, Annie knew exactly what she wanted, and she even told the paramedic to write down a list of her wishes in the ambulance on her way in to Accident and Emergency. Beside my name, she wrote 'October 4 – Today's reminder', and I truly hope I've rightfully assumed that she wanted me to read this passage from one of her favourite books, *Courage to Change*:

> *"Although we have our unique qualities, all hearts beat under the same skin. Your heart reaches out to mine as you share your story and your faith. I know that the part of myself which I share with you is taken to your heart. Today I will cherish our collective strength.*

"And I really feel that this message is meant for everyone sitting here today, united in our love for Annie. Thanks for listening and God bless you all."

As Guy came back to take his seat next to me, my heart swelled with love for him. We linked arms and listened to the rest of the service until it was time to leave. Andrea Bocelli and Sarah Brightman's 'Time To Say Goodbye' sung her out, causing many a guest to sob into their hankies. The words made it all the more real. Annie was gone from this world and we would never see her in the flesh again.

As we followed her coffin to its final resting place, I noticed that she would be laid beside her beloved husband George. And as we got closer still, I watched a pair of robins appear from the freshly dug plot, one with a juicy worm in its beak. Annie and George, I thought. Together at last.

Her son and daughter each threw in a rose, and one by one, Annie's blood family said their goodbyes and left the cemetery for drinks in the local pub.

But her spiritual family felt compelled to remain. One of

Annie's oldest friends in Al-Anon, Ronnie, who had phoned Guy with the news of her death, asked us to form a circle around her grave. Mousey Martha stood to my left, and a kind-looking woman who Guy seemed to know, positioned herself to my right.

With great authority, similar to that of Annie's, Ronnie began to speak.

"Each of us here is part of a circle of hope that is greater than any of our individual problems and differences. Let us join our hands in a circle and say the words of the Serenity Prayer together..."

Drawing great strength from each other, our collective voices grew evermore powerful as we repeated the words that had come to mean so much.

"God, grant me
the serenity to accept the things I cannot change,
the courage to change the things I can,
and the wisdom to know the difference."

I had once imagined that losing my Earth Angel teacher would be the saddest day of my life. But it wasn't. Something was lifting my soul up, far beyond a place of grief, and I knew, without a shadow of a doubt, that it was Annie. And I also believed for the very first time, in my heart of hearts, that no matter what the future held for me, everything was going to be just fine.

-End-

References

Two books have been mentioned in this fictional story, which are real in their existence. They are full of wisdom, truly inspirational and highly recommended by Jo.

These are:-

The Language of Letting Go, by Melody Beattie, published by Hazelden.

Courage to Change: one day at a time in Al-Anon II, Al-Anon Family Groups.

About The Author

Jo Barnard lives with her husband, two sons and rescue poodle, by the river of a small Essex town. In 2008, she gave up her fifteen-year career in marketing to pursue her passion for holistic living, and set up her wellbeing clinic, 'you-time', where she offers various treatments, teaches Reiki and meditation, and encourages others to step into their own personal power.

Her other passion is writing, and Jo has written for several well-known spiritual magazines in the form of articles, meditation CDs and card decks. Her self-help book, *Meditation Made Simple,* was published in 2012, and was later recorded as an audio book.

Jo has met some truly inspirational people with amazing stories along the way, which have roused the novelist in her. *To the Devil's Tune* is her first fictional offering, and was written in less than a month, as a tribute to her late friend.

Details of all Jo's work can be found at www.you-time.com

At Roundfire we publish great stories. We lean towards the spiritual and thought-provoking. But whether it's literary or popular, a gentle tale or a pulsating thriller, the connecting theme in all Roundfire fiction titles is that once you pick them up you won't want to put them down.